SHOOTER

Also by Walter Dean Myers

FICTION

CRYSTAL

THE DREAM BEARER

HANDBOOK FOR BOYS: A NOVEL

IT AIN'T ALL FOR NOTHIN'

MONSTER
2000 Michael L. Printz Award
1999 Coretta Scott King Author Honor Book
1999 National Book Award Finalist

THE MOUSE RAP

PATROL: AN AMERICAN SOLDIER IN VIETNAM
2003 Jane Addams Children's Book Award

THE RIGHTEOUS REVENGE OF ARTEMIS BONNER

SCORPIONS
A 1989 Newbery Honor Book

THE STORY OF THE THREE KINGDOMS

NONFICTION

ANGEL TO ANGEL: A MOTHER'S GIFT OF LOVE

BAD BOY: A MEMOIR

BROWN ANGELS: AN ALBUM OF PICTURES AND VERSE

I'VE SEEN THE PROMISED LAND: THE LIFE OF DR. MARTIN LUTHER KING, JR.

MALCOLM X: A FIRE BURNING BRIGHTLY

NOW IS YOUR TIME!: THE AFRICAN-AMERICAN STRUGGLE FOR FREEDOM
1992 Coretta Scott King Author Award

Walter Dean Myers

SHOOTER

Amistad
HarperTempest
An Imprint of HarperCollins*Publishers*

Shooter

Copyright © 2004 by Walter Dean Myers

www.harpertempest.com

Library of Congress Cataloging-in-Publication Data

Myers, Walter Dean, date

Shooter / Walter Dean Myers.— 1st ed.

p. cm.

Summary: Written in the form of interviews, reports, and journal entries, the story of three troubled teenagers ends in a tragic school shooting.

ISBN 0-06-029519-8 — ISBN 0-06-029520-1 (lib. bdg.)

[1. School violence—Fiction. 2. Family problems—Fiction. 3. Emotional problems—Fiction. 4. Bullies—Fiction. 5. Schools—Fiction.] I. Title.

PZ7.M992Sh 2004

[Fic]—dc22   2003015552

CIP

AC

Typography by R. Hult

4 5 6 7 8 9 10

❖

First Edition

To Bill Morris,
my friend for so many years

SHOOTER

Harrison County School Safety Committee

Threat Analysis Report

Submitted by:

Dr. Jonathan Margolies
Superintendent, Harrison County Board of Education

Dr. Richard Ewings
Senior County Psychologist

Special Agent Victoria Lash
F.B.I. Threat Assessment Analyst

Dr. Franklyn Bonner
Spectrum Group

Sheriff William Beach Mosley
Harrison County Criminal Bureau

Mission Statement

The Harrison County School Safety Committee, headed by Dr.
Jonathan Margolies, is to investigate public school safety using
interviews and all available records, with particular emphasis on
the tragic events of last April; and to analyze and assess all possible threats and dangers within the County's school community;
and to report to the Governor of this State any findings consistent
with imminent or possible threats to:

- Any student or group of students
- Any educator or administrator
- Any other person
- Any structure or building

It is understood by the members of the Safety Committee that the
generated report will not carry a prima facie legal obligation but
that it might be used in some legal capacity, and that all inter-
viewees must be informed of their Miranda rights.

Madison High School Incident Analysis
Report I—Interview with Cameron Porter
Submitted by Dr. Richard Ewings,
Senior County Psychologist

Cameron Porter is a seventeen-year-old African American youth who attended Madison High School in Harrison County. His grades ran in the high eighties and there is no indication, in his school records, of difficulty in social adjustment. He lives in a two-parent household and is the only child. The parental income is quite high, and there is no indication of deprivation.

Cameron has been advised that the interviews will not be privileged and that they can be subpoenaed for any subsequent legal action, but that the primary aim of the interviews is for analytical purposes. He has agreed to be interviewed in an effort to cooperate with the Analysis team and has signed a waiver to that effect.

He appeared at my office punctually, accompanied by his mother, who then left for another appointment. Cameron is a good-looking young man, neatly dressed, of medium to dark complexion. He seems reasonably comfortable and no more nervous than would be expected under the circumstances. A letter informing Cameron of his Miranda rights was drafted, signed by him, and put on file.

The initial taped interview began at 10:30 on the morning of October 24. This was six months after the incident at the high school.

Notes to transcriber:

- Please return all tapes to my office as soon as possible.
- Please indicate significant pauses or other voicings in the unedited draft of this report.

Richard Ewings

Dr. Richard Ewings

Richard Ewings: Good morning.

Cameron Porter: Good morning.

RE: Do you mind if I call you Cameron?

CP: Fine.

RE: Cameron, can we begin by you telling me something
about yourself? Where do you live? Who do you live
with? That sort of thing?

CP: Sure. I live over on Jewett Avenue. I live with my mom,
Elizabeth, and my father.

RE: Can you give me your father's name and tell me what
sort of work your parents do?

CP: My father's name is Norman. He does quality control for
Dyna-Rod Industries. They manufacture heavy
equipment, and they lease it to building contractors.
What he does is travel around and check out how the
leasing end of their business works. My mother works
for an office-supply company.

RE: What would heavy equipment consist of?

CP: Cranes, derricks, specialized vehicles.

RE: How would you describe how you get along with your
parents?

CP: Okay. Just normal I guess.

RE: Do you go out with them much? Are there family
conversations, say, around the dinner table?

CP: My father travels a lot. He's away about a week and a
half every month. Maybe more, I don't know. We sort

11

of—I wouldn't say that we talk a lot. I wouldn't say that we *don't* talk a lot, either. We go out—we used to go out to eat once a month. Arturo's. You know where that is?

RE: About a mile off 95, isn't it?

CP: Down from the mall.

RE: Right. That's a nice place. Good Italian food. Do you enjoy eating there?

CP: It's okay. No big deal. They like it.

RE: What kinds of things do you talk about at Arturo's? Actually, what kinds of things do you enjoy talking about with your parents?

CP: I guess we don't really talk that much. When we do talk—usually it's about something—maybe about their jobs or something. They talk about their jobs a lot. They're trying to—they have these goals they work on. You know, what they want to accomplish every year, that sort of thing.

RE: What do you think of their goals?

CP: Their goals? They're okay. They have things they want to do. Financial security—that sort of thing. They're, like, doing the right things.

RE: When you say they're doing the right things, do you mean that *you* think they're doing the right things?

CP: Yeah. Yes, I guess so.

RE: How would you describe your relationship with your

12

parents? Can you tell me how you think you get along with them, perhaps if there were different things you would have liked to have done with them than you were doing?

CP: They asked me that at the county office.

RE: And what did you say?

CP: I have a good relationship with my parents. They're okay.

RE: Cameron, I'm not trying to suggest you don't have a good relationship with your parents. I know that's always the cliché that people want to drag out. But I am trying to get as full a picture of you as I can. To know you, or to try to get to know you, I need to know about your relationships. With your parents, of course, and with Leonard. I'm sure you can understand that.

CP: Yeah. Yes.

RE: "Yeah" is fine here. Do you have any hobbies? Do you play an instrument? What do you do in your spare time?

CP: I play flute. I'm not great at it or anything. I wanted to play bass guitar. Once I rented one and I liked it, but I didn't keep it up. Mostly I sort of do what everybody else does. I like sports, music. Regular stuff.

RE: What kind of music do you listen to?

CP: It changes. People think you listen to one kind of music—that's crazy. You turn the radio on or you play your own stuff and that's what you do. There was a big thing in the paper about Satyricon, but it was like other kids talking, not me. I listen to them, but I'm not a real freak for them, and I'm not into any Fourth Reich number. That's why I agreed to talk with you, to get things straight.

RE: And I really appreciate it, Cameron. One of the things that I see on a regular basis is how the media can distort reality.

CP: I think I'm average. Pretty much average.

RE: You don't have an average IQ. You've been tested in the 140 range, which is very high. And on the test you were given, that's the top of the range, so I know you're above average in measurable intelligence. I scored about 15 points less than you did on that same test.

CP: It doesn't mean anything. I think it doesn't mean anything.

RE: I'm not sure. I don't think anybody is really sure about intelligence. Or at least intelligence that's measured on tests. . . . What do you think Leonard would say about your IQ score?

CP: He made a big deal of it. He was into that kind of thing. A lot of people are, really. Some people say that they're not, but then you hear them talking about who is smart or who isn't smart. It's the same way they talk about who can play ball or who has the best car. It's always about comparisons. Kids measure each other and then pretend they're not doing it.

RE: How about your parents? They must have been proud of your grades.

CP: They expected me to do okay. They're not into academics. With them it's like always knowing what's the smart thing to do. My father always says that you can have a high IQ and still be stupid.

RE: What's your father's goal in life?

CP: One goal? I don't know. Maybe to have everybody talking about how smart he is. Something like that.

RE: And that was okay with you?

CP: I don't think about it that much. Yeah, it's okay.

RE: You ever just "hang out" with your father?

CP: He plans things—he doesn't just—he's not a casual sort of guy. Neither of my parents are. They're sort of intense. They're not, like, super intense, but they're pretty intense. They don't hang out.

RE: That describes a lot of parents.

CP: I guess.

RE: You look more like your father or your mother?

CP: More like my mom's side of the family. Not so much like her.

RE: When did you first meet Leonard?

CP: We were in the third grade together, but I didn't meet him then. I mean, we were in the same class. We figured that out after we became friends, but we weren't friends at first. We were in about three grades together without

15

ever knowing each other that much.

RE: How did you become friends with him?

CP: We more or less got together in our sophomore year. I was trying out for the basketball team. He came to all the tryouts just to watch. I didn't make the team and I felt pretty bad. One day we were walking home together—he lives near Fairmount—and Len was kidding me about not making the team. Actually he kidded me a lot, but he had a way of almost putting you down but smiling as he did it. Do you know what I mean?

RE: No, not really.

CP: He'd say things like, "Hey, Cam, you really stunk the place up." But he'd be smiling and you felt—I felt that he was putting me down, but not in a mean way. Like when they made the final cuts, I got that far, and I wasn't on the team and my father found out and started putting me down. Len wasn't like that.

RE: Your father was upset that you didn't make the team?

CP: You're making like it was a big deal. It wasn't.

RE: I'm sorry. Why don't you tell me about it?

CP: My father used to be like all-world or something. He's got a scrapbook, trophies, the whole nine yards. He played basketball in the Army and then professional ball in Europe after he got out. He's strong and that's his game. He comes right after you and muscles you away from the basket. Then after he hacks you to death, he starts talking about how you play like a girl, that sort of thing.

RE: How does that make you feel?

CP: How do you think it makes me feel? You think it makes me feel good?

RE: Obviously it doesn't. So you and Len, I think that's what you call him, became friends around that time?

CP: Yeah, a little after that. About a week later I was home and my father said that he was coming to the game that weekend and he hoped I played well. I told him I hadn't made the team, and he said I was on it. He said he had "fixed it." Then I got called down to the gym the next day and the coach told me I was on the team. Some of the guys said that they had put this kid named Boyd off the team so I could play, and they knew my father had something to do with it. I felt like crap. That blew it for me as far as the guys on the team were concerned. They had been my friends, more or less, but after that happened, I didn't hang with them anymore.

RE: You're saying that the basketball incident cut down on the number of friends you had?

CP: Friends on the basketball team, anyway.

RE: Do you have a lot of other friends?

CP: I don't go around counting them. But I don't go out looking for people to party with. Is that what you mean?

RE: You have a girlfriend?

17

CP: No one in particular. I figured I'd wait for college. I don't drive, either.

RE: Not driving in Harrison County can cramp your style. You took driver's ed?

CP: Yeah. I was thinking of getting a wreck—a used car—but my father said it would be more trouble than useful. He said I should wait for college.

RE: What does he drive?

CP: ML 500. Mercedes with the wheel on the right side. It's cool.

RE: And showy.

CP: Yeah.

RE: What did you think of Madison? A good school academically?

CP: It's okay. It's the only high school I ever went to, so I can't compare it with anything else. It doesn't look like an inner-city school or anything like that. You know, you see those schools on television or in the movies and they look rough.

RE: It's one of the biggest schools I've seen. The parking lot is bigger than the high school I went to. Over a thousand students I think.

CP: It's pretty big.

RE: Did you have many friends in the school?

CP: It depends on what you mean by friends. Everybody talks about friends, but they don't define what that

18

means. If you mean did I hang out with a lot of different people, well, I didn't. And then, when me and Len started hanging out, I guess it was just me and him and a few other kids. And mostly it was me and him. He drove me to school a lot of the time.

RE: You played basketball. Are many of your friends athletes?

CP: No.

RE: That's a little unusual, isn't it? Ballplayers have a tendency to hang out together.

CP: You're trying to fit me in, right? I have to be either a ballplayer or a loner, or what? You need to fit me in someplace, right?

RE: What I'm trying to figure out is who you are. It's fine if you don't fit any of the categories I've mentioned. But I would like to know, at least, how you picture yourself.

CP: In the first place, I stopped playing on the school team. And I see myself as an ordinary guy. No big deal. If this thing hadn't happened, you would never have heard of me. And that would have been good, as far as I'm concerned. I don't want to stand out. I just want to get on with my life the best I can.

RE: How did Len see you?

CP: He said—he saw me as somebody who was all right.

RE: Do you remember any time that he actually told you what he thought of you?

CP: He said I was all right. He said I didn't have to do

19

anything to be all right, I just was.

RE: What do you think that meant?

CP: Just what he said, that I was okay.

RE: You ever meet his parents? Did he seem to get along with them?

CP: I think he got along with them the same as I got along with mine. More or less. Or maybe not, I don't know. My parents are always going somewhere. That's, like, their thing. You know, they're always on the way to the airport or to some meeting. And my father is, like—he can be with you and talking to you but not with you at the same time. But he's not like Len's father. Mr. Gray, Len's father, is like super macho, and he belongs to civic groups—stuff like that. He's sort of like "pals."

RE: What do you mean by that?

CP: Like, he's going to talk to you like you're his age and you're old friends.

RE: Did Len like his father?

CP: I don't think that Len liked anybody. I mean, when I think back on it, I don't think he liked anybody.

RE: He liked you, didn't he?

CP: Yes.

RE: What made you different for Len?

CP: I don't know.

RE: Were you always comfortable in your relationship with him?

20

CP: I don't think you always have to be comfortable in your relationship with somebody. You just have to get along with them.

RE: I think that's true. I also think it's a good observation. Have you seen Len's father since the incident?

CP: No.

RE: According to the records, you had an unpleasant experience at one of Mr. Gray's civic groups?

CP: It wasn't a big deal. I know I mentioned it to the psychiatrist over at the center and she made a big deal of it and that's how it got written down as a big deal. I guess it was written down as a big deal.

RE: One of the dangers in these interviews is that the interviewer changes the importance of the answers. I try to be careful, but it's always a possibility that I might misinterpret something. At least I'm usually aware that it's a possibility. So, you've rethought the incident at the shooting club and you don't think that it was significant?

CP: No.

RE: There was a racial component to the incident. That brings up the question of how you got along with the white kids at Madison.

CP: I don't see how they're connected. One thing happened at a club; the other part, getting along with white kids in school, is separate.

RE: Some people might make a connection.

21

CP: Whatever.

RE: But you got along just fine?

CP: Fine. No problem. They're pretty much a middle-of-the-road group. A lot of them give themselves names like liberal or conservative, but they mostly think alike. They've got a political-correctness thing going on. There are things you can put people down for, and things you can't put them down for. I never got any grief because I was black.

RE: What kinds of things did kids get put down for?

CP: It depended.

RE: On what?

CP: On what group you were with. If you weren't in the jock group and you were with a bunch of jocks, then maybe they would put you down. If you weren't into the drum-and-bass group, then they would put you down for that. And some kids just didn't—I would say that Len and I didn't fit into many groups. I'm not saying that as an excuse for anything. I'm just saying it because that's the way it was.

RE: Going back to the incident with Len's father's civic group. Do you mind telling me about it? I know it's not a big deal to you, but again, I'm trying to understand what Len was like.

CP: Well, Len kind of laughed it off too. Almost like he did when I didn't make the basketball team. He called me one Friday and asked me if I wanted to go shooting up at his father's camp. It wasn't really his father's camp, just a camp where his father shot sometimes. I thought it sounded cool, so I said okay.

The camp was about five miles, maybe six, out of town. There were these guys, all white, who talked about guns and about how the country was getting too soft and letting too many immigrants in, that sort of thing. They have a camp and a shooting range. Mr. Gray asked me if I wanted to shoot. I said okay. So I shot. It was cool. I used a rifle that wasn't automatic. They were trying to get small groups. Some guys could get groups you could cover with a quarter.

RE: What do you mean by groups?

CP: You set up and shoot three shots at the target. If you hit the bull's-eye, or even if you miss, the shots should be close together. That's how you zero your piece in. If you're a good shot, your bullets hit close together even if the rifle is off a little.

RE: Okay.

CP: Then we all got in a line and walked along in a row— they called it a skirmish line—and there were pop-up targets. You couldn't shoot at anything too close—they had to be at least fifteen yards in front of you—and the targets would pop up from the ground. That was fun. Most of the targets were like comic-book figures of bad

23

guys with guns pointing at you. A few were women with bags of groceries and you weren't supposed to shoot them. You had to make a quick decision. Then one popped up and it was Martin Luther King, Jr., holding a gun and they all shot him down.

RE: That was supposed to be a joke?

CP: I guess.

RE: That was pretty rough.

CP: No big deal. I didn't agree with it, but it was no big deal. You don't have to like everything that everybody does.

RE: So as a black man you didn't mind them shooting at Dr. King's image.

[Here there is a prolonged pause.]

CP: I didn't like it.

RE: Why?

CP: I don't know. Maybe because I knew I was putting me being black on the sideline. Only I really couldn't, you know.

RE: It had to be painful.

CP: You're not black.

RE: No, but there have been times in my life when I've had to put aside who I was. And every time I did put my own self, my own feelings, aside, it was painful.

CP: I told my father about it.

RE: What did he say?

24

CP: He said that's how business was done. He said people test you to see if you can stay focused on business or if you're going to go off on some civil-rights kick and throw away the business.

RE: And you said?

CP: Nothing. You don't argue with my father.

RE: But if you could have argued with your father, what would you have said?

CP: I don't know.

RE: You want to take a guess?

CP: Maybe that I felt a little ashamed of myself.

RE: Ashamed?

CP: Maybe that's the way I feel most of the time.

RE: Do you feel that way now?

CP: A little.

RE: Do you need some time? You want to take a break?

CP: I'm okay.

RE: Cameron, sometimes life doesn't let us feel good about ourselves. And that's true if you're seventeen or forty-three.

CP: I guess.

RE: Speaking of your age, I noticed that you were only sixteen in your senior year. Did you skip a grade?

CP: No, I learned to read early—when I was four—and my father got me into the first grade at five.

RE: Really? Do you think that bothered you? I mean, socially?

25

CP: Not at first. Maybe not at all. I'm not sure.

RE: You don't have to have a sure answer for everything.

CP: That's good.

RE: Okay. Okay. Cameron, I'd like to ask you some personal questions. Some of them might not be particularly comfortable, but I'd like you to do the best you can on all of them. I noticed that you were taking medication for depression. You want to tell me about the depression, and how the medication helped or didn't help?

CP: It started with the church thing. When that happened, I started taking the medicine. It was prescribed by Dr. Brendel. I went to her for six months.

RE: What's the church thing?

CP: You don't have that?

RE: No.

CP: Oh, okay. Len and I were arrested for vandalizing a church. My parents and his mother got together, and they arranged for us to have psychiatric interviews. Then they had talks with the church and it ended with us cleaning up the mess we made and us taking counseling. The prescriptions were part of the counseling.

RE: I didn't know about the church. Maybe it's here somewhere. Why don't you tell me about it?

CP: It was Len's idea. We were down at Al's Diner off the ramp—you know where that is? It's near that warehouse where you can rent storage bins?

RE: I think so.

CP: And it was right before Christmas. Len had this theory that if something is supposed to be good, it should be righteous. That's his word, "righteous." Which more or less means true and without any B.S. We saw the crèche in front of the church with a little blond Mary and a little blue-eyed Joseph and a little Jesus surrounded by the animals. Len said that they weren't dealing with Jesus at all, just the commercial part of the holiday. He was really pissed with the church. We went to the front door to look in. I didn't think it was going to matter much, so I went in with him. The front door was locked, but we went around to the side entrance and got in. The church was cool. It was a Catholic church with all the statues and whatnot. Len started writing on the walls with a Magic Marker. He wrote—in really big letters—"GOD DOES NOT LIVE HERE!" It was just a spur-of-the-moment thing.

RE: Did you write on the walls too?

CP: Yeah, I wrote, "JESUS WOULDN'T EVEN RENT THIS SPACE." Then we left and we went to his house and watched television for a while. Len said that the only program on television that wasn't a lie was the Yule log burning.

Eventually they found out who did it and we got

picked up, the whole nine, and ended up with a court date, which meant that we had to show up in court on a certain day. But before that day came, like I said, we both went to psychiatrists who gave us prescriptions for antidepressant medicines. I think Len got a different one than I did.

RE: Were you depressed?

CP: I don't know. Maybe a little.

RE: Why did you go to a psychiatrist?

CP: The lawyer Len's dad hired told us we should and who to go to.

RE: And you showed up in court with a whole story about how you were depressed?

CP: Yeah.

RE: How did that make you feel?

CP: I finessed it.

RE: What does that mean?

CP: I didn't feel good about it, but I got through it. Sometimes that's what I do. Just try to get through the moment.

RE: What did your parents say?

CP: They said I was stupid. They were trying to make something happen for me and I was too stupid to see it.

RE: Do your parents believe in God?

CP: Yeah.

RE: Were they disappointed that you vandalized a church?

28

CP: I don't think they ever asked me about that. About the church part.

CE: What did they ask you about?

CP: Mostly about why I would do something so stupid.

RE: What medication was prescribed for you?

CP: I don't remember.

RE: I can find that out. How did they make you feel? Did you take them as they were prescribed?

CP: Yeah, I did. They made me feel okay. Mostly because it was like I had a real problem, that it wasn't all just made up or something. I mean, if a doctor gave you the prescription, it meant something was wrong.

RE: I suppose. That meant a lot to you, a formal idea that something was wrong?

CP: Yeah, it did.

RE: Did you think you were depressed before you started taking the pills?

CP: Sometimes I was.

RE: What does that mean to you? Being depressed?

CP: Being down. Sad, I guess.

RE: And did the pills make you feel less sad?

CP: Sort of. Yes.

RE: And then what happened?

CP: As Len said, we were formally "nutcases" and they dropped the charges in return for a promise that we would clean up the church and be cool.

RE: Do you see yourself as a "nutcase"?

CP: No, that was what he called us. Len. He said as long as we were nutcases and juveniles, they couldn't touch us.

RE: And all you did was to write on the wall that Jesus wouldn't rent the space?

[Here there is a long silence.]

RE: And all you did was to write on the wall that Jesus wouldn't rent the space?

CP: We wrote other stuff. Some obscene stuff.

RE: And obviously you feel pretty bad about that. Did you feel bad about it then?

CP: Yes.

RE: Then why did you write it?

CP: I didn't want to disappoint him.

RE: Len?

CP: Len.

RE: Because you were his friend?

CP: Because we were in it together. That means a lot. You're in something with someone.

RE: You admired him?

CP: In a way.

RE: Did you ever fantasize about being him? About being Len?

CP: No.

RE: What did Len look like?

CP: A regular-looking guy. He didn't have a hard look. You

30

wouldn't think he was a jock or anything. He had dark eyes, regular features. Kind of large eyes, I guess. He would look down at the ground when he was talking to you, or away from you, and then when he finished he would look up at you.

RE: Did you ever think of being Len's brother?

CP: No.

RE: Did you ever think of holding him? Putting your arms around him?

CP: I wondered when you were going to get to that. It was in one of the papers that we were "really close." No, I never thought of kissing him or any other guy. I'm not gay, man.

RE: Does it bother you that I ask?

CP: If I say "yes," does that make me a closet gay?

RE: No, and I think I can appreciate how you feel. I'm not trying to trick you into anything. But I want to ask all the obvious questions. You went a long way with Len. You did things with him that most people don't do. I'm trying to figure out the circumstances that led to those things. Did you ever question your relationship with Len?

CP: No. Not before the shootings. Now I do.

RE: Cameron, when we look at Len's behavior, a pattern emerges. Now, maybe that pattern is something we're imposing on his life. I know that happens even though we're supposed to be professionals. You mentioned earlier that we get locked into certain ideas. There's reason to believe that when Len went to the school that day, he went there expressly to die. In other words, it was an elaborate way of committing suicide. Have you ever thought of suicide?

CP: Before it happened, I used to think of suicide sometimes. Now I think about it all the time. I think if I could pull it off, my parents would be a lot happier. They could deal with it. I've really cost them a lot of money. They'd probably come up with a timetable when they would get over it. It's not like I want to die. It's more like I just want to get this whole thing over with. That's why I don't mind—or maybe why I answer all the questions you're asking. I don't think any of this is going to do any good. It's not going to bring anybody back to life. Is it?

RE: If you were going to reverse things, go back in time so to speak—where would you start?

CP: I don't know. I'm so sorry about all of it. I just screwed up everybody.

RE: Do you need a moment?

CP: No.

RE: It's okay to show your emotions, Cameron. Crying is no big deal. It's just another way that humans have to express themselves. Did you have a chance to talk to the doctor who prescribed your antidepressants?

CP: I talked to her, but I was so down it didn't matter. I was really ashamed. The kids at school really dumped on me.

RE: And your parents.

CP: My father was so pissed. He grabbed me and pushed my head against the wall and just held me there. He had his fist balled up like he was going to hit me, but he didn't. He held me there for a long while and my mother was begging him not to hit me. He said he was ashamed to have me for a son.

RE: How did that make you feel? Him saying that?

CP: Terrible. In a way I was used to it from him, but I still felt terrible. Then he went on about how I could either make something of myself in life or be something that people accidentally stepped in. It didn't take much to figure out what he thought I was.

RE: Did your father ever hit you?

CP: No.

RE: Never?

CP: No. Sometimes I dreamed he would hit me.

RE: You dreamed he would hit you? Did you want him to hit you?

CP: In a way I did. Just so I wouldn't feel so bad. If he hit me, I could just take it and get over it. But when he got on my case, kept telling me I was crap, it was like I

33

couldn't get over it and didn't have any place to get away from it.

RE: What did Len think about the incident?

CP: For him it was like a symbolic thing. You know, against the church and all. He always hated the symbols that we had to live by.

RE: Had to live by? What does that mean?

CP: The American flag. The church. The physical church buildings. You know how they try to make them look so traditional. He always thought that the buildings had become symbols and didn't have a real religious meaning anymore. Whenever he saw a symbol, he wanted to crush it. Or he would just laugh at it.

RE: Did you admire him for this?

CP: I don't know. At least he was honest. I liked him for a lot of things he did. Even people who didn't like him copied him.

RE: Did you see Len as a kind of symbol? Was he the rebel, the outsider?

CP: He wasn't that much of a rebel. I think if he could have fit in, he would have. Most of the things he did seemed normal. It wasn't outside stuff, really.

RE: Vandalizing the church seemed normal to you?

CP: It sounds stupid now, but it didn't seem that way when we were doing it.

RE: You said before that they—I assume that "they" are the

police—found out that you did it. How did they find out?

CP: Len went to the parish house and told the guy who was living there—I think he took care of the building, he wasn't a priest or anything—that he thought he heard noises coming from the church, that maybe one of the prophets was calling out for help. So when the guy checked it out and called the police, they eventually got around to calling Len to find out what he had heard or seen. He figured he might as well give himself up because they would find out sooner or later that it was him. So he did.

RE: So he gave himself up. And he gave you up too?

CP: No, the next day it was in the paper. The *Herald*. Some reporter named Michelle Garcia had written up this whole fantasy about a cult and that Len was part of it. A couple of kids brought it over to me and showed me what my friend was doing. They were all saying it was disgusting. The paper said that there were at least two people involved and that Len wouldn't say who the other person was. I knew the kids were looking at me. Mr. Washington, the principal, saw me in the hall and asked me if I knew anything about it. I said yes.

RE: You know, it sounds to me as if you wanted to be caught. That you wanted to be caught and that Len wanted to be caught.

CP: Whatever.

RE: What do you think about that?

CP: Everybody wants to explain me and Len. You might as well do it too.

RE: Well, let me ask you right out. Did you want to be caught?

CP: No.

RE: What did you want?

CP: I wanted it to be over. I didn't want to drag it out. It was like waiting to get shot or something. Just get it over.

RE: You said everybody wants to explain you and Len. You're still very protective of him, aren't you?

CP: I don't know what you mean by that.

RE: You don't know what I mean? Okay. There was an incident in school, and it resulted in Len being suspended for a week. Do you remember that?

CP: It started over nothing. There was this girl, she was one of the Fancy Fart set. She had a fast mouth but she never really had anything to say. What she was about was putting people down. And she was supposed to be so foxy that you couldn't say anything to her. If you did put her down, she wouldn't know it. She was stupid.

One day she just got on Len's case big-time. He was wearing his hat. He wore his hat in school a lot. And she came over and started getting on his case for that. He told her to take a walk. There were some jock types around, so she sat down right at Len's table and started talking about how she wasn't scared of him and everything, and the jocks, they were at the next table, started laughing. She pushed up on Len, got her face right into his, and he said something to her and some spit came out of his mouth. He didn't mean to spit on her, but he was talking and some came out. She slapped him. Then he slapped her back. Then two jocks jumped him and started punching him out and some teachers broke it up. Then this girl's boyfriend, Brad, heard about it and said he was going to beat up Len. We were in the hallway later, outside the Media Center, and her boyfriend and some other jocks surrounded us.

RE: How did you get involved in it?

CP: I was just with him. He had told me about it but we weren't talking about it at the time. He had just read this book and he was all excited about it. Len read a lot. He was really smart. Anyway, I was with him, and they surrounded us and started calling us names.

RE: What kinds of names?

CP: The usual names. Faggots. Pussies. They started slapping us around. Not hard. Just to show that they could. They told us to get down on our knees and beg for mercy. We didn't do that and they forced us down. Some girls came by and told them to let us up, but then some other girls started laughing. Mr. Anders came into the hall, and the jocks all started walking away. One of them pointed at us and told Mr. Anders that we were trying to have sex with them. Mr. Anders knew better, but he didn't say anything. He's the baseball coach, and he lets the jocks get away with everything. Then we got up and left the school.

RE: Where did you go?

CP: We went downtown. Len was pissed. He was really pissed and hurt. I was too. He was just about shaking, he was so mad. He couldn't think straight and asked me if I wanted to go with him to get something for his nerves. I said okay. He went back to the school. He was driving. I waited in the car for him and he went into the school and came out. When I was sitting in the car, I felt I was just where I wanted to be, outside looking at the place, not inside dealing with it.

RE: Did that bring the two of you closer together?

CP: No. I just thought maybe I shouldn't hang out with him. Some of the black guys in school started asking me how come I was tight with a white faggot. I didn't want to stick up for him.

RE: Why? I thought by this time you were friendly with him?

CP: I was, but I didn't want to be pushed around and called names by people when he did something they didn't like. Anyway, I sort of didn't want to be against the black guys in the school. There were only a handful of

us and we sort of stuck together. Two of the main jocks
were black.

RE: How did any of this lead to Len's getting suspended?

CP: He was really mad—not like in his head, but in his
body. His shoulders were shaking and his hands were
trembling. There was a kid in school who was taking
some drug, I think it was Librium or Prozac,
something. A lot of the kids were on something. That
was what Len went back to school for. Len asked the
kid to lend him the prescription. He took it in to a
pharmacy to a girl he knew who worked there to have
it filled.

RE: For himself?

CP: Yeah. He needed a sedative, his head was so messed
up. Anyway, we got it filled, but then the pharmacist
checked all the prescriptions that night and called the
kid's doctor, who called the kid's parents, et cetera, et
cetera. The kid ratted Len out, naturally, and that got
Len suspended for a week.

RE: Was the incident—I guess you would call it bullying—
did it end with that one occurrence?

CP: It never ends. You know, everybody gets sorted out after
a while. And if you get a label—that you're easy—then
they're going to find you. They push you and they push
you, just to see how far they can go, I think. I don't
know.

39

RE: What happened next?

CP: A couple of days after Len got back to school, Brad came up to him and said he was going to kick his ass. So Len said how come he didn't fight him fair and square, instead of with all of his friends around. They travel in packs. You see one jock, you see a pack of them. Brad cracked up on that, because he knew he could beat Len. He said he would meet Len after school on the football field. It was about nine o'clock—we had just started school. Len told me to come with him in the afternoon. I didn't want to go, but I didn't want to say no to Len either.

Anyway, I didn't see him most of the day and I thought he had just left school. But at three o'clock he was there. About nine jocks went to the football field, and I was pretty sure we were both going to get beat up. Len was wearing his long coat—he looked like a cowboy. One of those old-time cowboys. Anyway, so Brad shows up—

RE: Brad Williams?

CP: Yeah. Brad grabbed Len by the collar, and Len just stood there smiling. The other jocks were telling Brad to knock the smirk off of Len's face. Brad slapped Len, but Len still didn't move and I could see he didn't know what to do. One of the other jocks pushed me toward Len. Pushed me in the back. I turned and looked at him, and

40

he got into my face and started calling me names. I turned and faced him and I think he wasn't sure whether he could take me or not. He was about my height and build. He just looked at me, and I thought he was going to take a swing at me or something.

RE: How did you feel at that time?

CP: It was like it was my job or something. He was supposed to stand there and make me feel bad, and my job was to stand there and take it.

RE: Were you afraid of an actual physical confrontation? Were you afraid of being hurt?

CP: No, I don't get afraid. I just get this sense of panic. Like everything's falling apart inside.

RE: Did he actually hit you?

CP: No. I think he wanted to, but then he said I was just a punk and he walked away. Then Brad pushed Len and said he wasn't worth wasting his time over.

I went with Len back to his car, and he thanked me for coming. When we got into the car, he asked me if I knew why he was thanking me. I said because if I hadn't been there, they might have jumped him. He said no, that if I hadn't been there he would have had to waste Brad. Then he opened his coat and pulled out the Ruger. I didn't even know he had it on him.

RE: The Ruger? That's a gun?

CP: Yeah, I had fired it once. It was his father's and it was

41

usually locked up. His father kept his pistols locked up and most of the ammo. But there was always something laying around. Len handled that really well. I thought Len had played it cool.

RE: You think that the fact that he didn't shoot him was a good thing?

CP: Yeah. I don't think . . . sometimes I daydream about getting back at people, but it stops there.

RE: Len showed restraint, but he was clearly thinking about shooting Brad at that time.

CP: Brad was clearly thinking about beating him up, too.

RE: How did you feel about Len having the gun?

CP: It was okay. It gave him power, even if he didn't use it. The whole thing with Brad was having power. Even Brad's girlfriend had a kind of power. She was always made up like a model or something and telling other girls how they should dress or what kind of makeup they should wear. That's power. Teachers have power.

RE: Cameron, you're an intelligent young man, and we both understand that. And we both understand that in a civilized society, guns are not the source of real power.

CP: You can say that. It makes sense and everything, but it mostly makes sense on paper. Some guy punching you out just because he can isn't real power, but it feels like it if he's standing in front of you. Or if somebody sits behind you in class and just keeps kicking the back of your chair and you don't want to turn around and face him, then he's got a kind of power over you. And that's real, man. Guns are real power. We wouldn't be here if they weren't.

RE: Len isn't here.

CP: He didn't really want to be, either.

RE: Did he ever talk to you about not being here?

[There is a significant pause here.]

RE: Cameron? Did Len ever talk to you about suicide?

CP: He mentioned it. No big deal.

RE: How did he mention it?

[Here there is another pause.]

CP: He said it was the ultimate power. Like being God.

RE: Can you elaborate on that?

CP: That was it. You're looking for comic-book conversations? People sitting around talking about dark things?

RE: What did you talk about mostly? Do you need something to drink?

CP: Scotch and soda.

RE: You drink?

CP: No.

RE: You ever take drugs?

CP: I'm not a head. I've tried weed. No big deal.

RE: What is a big deal to you?

CP: Not much, I guess.

RE: What did you and Len talk about?

CP: Whatever was going on. We didn't have an agenda.
School. Our parents. Other kids. Whatever.

RE: I assume Len met your parents. What did he think of
them?

CP: *[laughter]* He thought they were fascists. He thought all
parents were fascists. First, they're like dictators. They
give you all this talk about America being a democracy,
and equality—stuff like that. Then when you go home,
you find yourself living in a dictatorship. You don't have
any say about your life. They can punish you or tell you
to leave the room. We're all supposed to be capitalists,
but they control your finances down to the penny.
You're supposed to have First Amendment rights,
freedom of speech and all that, but they can just tell you
to shut up. When you're really young, you think all
that's fine, but later on you realize it sucks big-time.

RE: And you don't see the compensations? You don't see
that your parents support you? They feed you and clothe
you? That doesn't mean anything to you?

CP: How does that make me different from a dog or a cat?

RE: You're too intelligent not to see the difference, and I'm
too intelligent to play that little game. So—do you think
we can go on with the interview?

CP: Yeah.

RE: Did Len like your parents?

CP: He never really met them.

44

RE: He never came to your house?

CP: He came to my house, but my parents are hard to meet. One time he came over and Mom had this architect over. She was—her dream is to have this indoor pool. We have a big place. So she wanted to have the pool built in the garage so that you could enter from the outside or from the house. The garage is attached. So Len is over, and she starts asking Len about how he thinks the pool should look and whether or not it should be lit from inside the pool or just have overhead lights. And naturally she's telling him how much it's all going to cost. That's what she always does. She makes a lot of money and she wants people to know that.

RE: Isn't that a kind of power?

CP: I thought you were against power.

RE: I'm not against power that doesn't hurt people. Do you resent your mother making a lot of money?

CP: No.

RE: So what did Len think of your parents? Did he just say they were fascists and leave it at that?

CP: All he knew was that she was going to put the pool in. That and how much the pool cost. I think what he said was something like "How do they know they're black?" Something like that.

RE: What was that supposed to mean?

CP: I think he meant that they were trying to be something

they weren't. They were putting on this big show. My father's always talking about "making the smart move," and she's always talking about how much money she's spending. Even when we're just home together.

RE: Your parents have made some public remarks about Len. Do you know what they thought of him? Let's put it this way—you said he didn't really get to meet them. Did they meet him?

CP: They put him in a category. You know how adults want to put kids in a category. This kid is smart. This kid is this. This kid is that. But what you really are to them is "kid." And that's the main category. That means you're not much of anything. Whatever they think when they think of the word "kid" is what you are. When he started wearing black all the time, my father noticed it and said it was funny.

RE: When who started wearing black? Len? When Len was wearing black?

CP: He started wearing dark clothes. And a dark hat.

RE: Why?

CP: So he didn't have to do superficial things like match colors or try to dress cool. You know, half the school day is spent looking to see how everyone is dressed or talking about it.

RE: Did you wear black too?

CP: I toned down a little, not all the way.

46

RE: Part of how teenaged boys dress is in an effort to impress girls. Did you and Len talk about girls much?

CP: We talked about girls. Do you mean did we talk about having sex with girls? Yeah, we did. We didn't have girlfriends. We weren't staying away from girls, but we weren't into that social thing. Sometimes we were called nerds, or bangers, and I guess we were. We weren't gay or anything like that.

RE: Bangers? I've never heard that expression.

CP: That means you're so out of it, you should just go bang your head against the wall.

RE: That's pretty harsh.

CP: Welcome to Madison High.

RE: How much bullying went on at Madison?

CP: It was pretty constant. Once you became a target, they kept zeroing in on you. Did you ever see that video game where the guy tries to run across the screen, hiding behind rocks and stuff? And every time you shoot him, he stops and changes direction? If you shoot him enough times, he goes back and forth like a real jerk. That's what it was like sometimes at Madison. Everywhere you turned, somebody was saying something or doing something. It got pretty intense.

RE: And that made you feel—?

CP: You like that, right? You want me to say that it made me feel really bad and that puts me into the right category.

47

Kid felt really bad because of being bullied in school and reacted badly. That's what you want me to say?

RE: I think what I'm doing is trying my best to understand how you feel. I'm asking you questions and looking for answers. I don't want to put words in your mouth or create your thoughts. Why don't you tell me what I should think about the bullying?

[Here there is a long pause.]

RE: Would you like to end this session?

CP: Would I have to come back again?

RE: I have a few more questions.

CP: About the bullying. There are different parts to it. There's the part where someone is pushing you around, or throwing your books on the ground, that sort of thing. Another part is when you're not being bullied and you're still not dealing with other kids. Mostly the whole thing is how you feel about yourself. If you feel like you can be punked out, then that's where it is. You're punked out even when nobody's around.

RE: You want to explain that a little more?

CP: Say a kid is small. Well, you would think he would get picked on. But what happens really is that the kids who bully other kids sort of test them out. Then they find they can push you around and you, like, belong to them. Especially if you don't hang with a crowd.

RE: So being socially isolated is part of the process. But

didn't you and Len have a club of some sort? The papers made a big thing of that.

CP: Ordo Saggitae? There were only five of us in it. The papers played on it like they played on the idea that we all had super IQs and had all gone dark. That wasn't true.

RE: Tell me about the club.

CP: It was just a club. A lot of kids start clubs or bands or secret societies. Usually they don't last more than a week or so. Or if they last longer, it's just more or less a name. Ordo Saggitae means "Order of the Arrow," and it was cool. I liked it. There weren't any rules, or oaths or initiations, just five guys—actually four guys and Carla— who were going to do things together. We never actually did much, but we had a few meetings. It more or less broke up after Len and Carla fell out.

RE: Len had a girlfriend?

CP: I told you he wasn't gay.

RE: What happened with the girl?

CP: Len wasn't gay, but none of us had girls because we weren't into a social thing. There were some girls I liked. There weren't many black girls in the school, and some of the jocks—some of the black jocks—went out with white girls.

RE: Was the race of the girls important to you?

CP: No, but if you're going to start asking some girl to go

out with you and if you have to get your nerve up—and I did—then you look around for somebody a lot like you so she won't have so many reasons to say no. It just happened that most of my friends were white. And in a way that put me on the outside of some things. Len said he wasn't into Carla that much, but for a while, maybe a week or two, he was all about her. She's got, like, another side to her that only heads and freaks have, but she wasn't a head or a freak. One time in English the teacher, Mrs. Clift, was getting off on *Macbeth* and talking about how great Shakespeare was. Right in the middle of the whole thing Carla raised her hand and asked Mrs. Clift if she knew that Shakespeare was dead. Everybody laughed, and Mrs. Clift went on about how great works make the authors immortal. Then Carla said no, the authors aren't immortal, they die like they're supposed to, and we should just appreciate their work and move on.

The thing was that she said it so seriously and so dry that it shook Mrs. Clift. Some jerks tried to make a joke of it afterward, mostly sucking up to Mrs. Clift, but Carla had got over for just that moment. I was impressed, and I mentioned it to Len and it knocked him over. It really did, and from then on I think he was sweating Carla.

RE: Did he know that she had impressed you?

CP: Yeah, I told him.

50

RE: So he and Carla went out together?

CP: No, they didn't go out, they just hung out. She liked him, too, and she went dark. She wore dark mascara and black lipstick, which on her looked good. When we started Ordo Saggitae, she was the only girl we asked in. I thought eventually we would ask more girls to join, but she was the first.

RE: I'm a little confused. You mentioned wearing black. Now you're talking about "going dark." Are we talking about the same thing here?

CP: Wearing black is wearing black. Going dark is moving away from all those light things that seem to get some people through their day. Getting away from symbols and all that puffed-up way of living.

RE: Puffed up?

CP: Suits and ties. Passing down judgments on people. That's all puffed up. It's filled with air. Nothing.

RE: You said Len and Carla broke up?

CP: Yeah, right after the turtle thing.

RE: What was that about?

CP: Len and I had done some shooting. We got to the point where we were shooting a lot. His father was an ex-Ranger and belonged to the Patriots group and also a shooting range. He got us permits to shoot on weekends.

RE: Okay. What kinds of weapons did you shoot?

CP: Lots of different weapons. Len liked to shoot different weapons. You could borrow them from the range. His father owned a couple of Rugers, nice pieces, a target rifle that was sweet that he only let us shoot once, an old M14, and a Kalashnikov. When we started the club, Len invited Carla to shoot, and she did but I don't think she liked it. She was a good shot, though. The range max was a hundred yards and she could shoot okay at that distance. She could even get a really tight group if she used a sling. The big deal was to shoot in between your heartbeats so the piece wouldn't jerk. Especially if you were using a sling.

RE: You liked shooting?

CP: Yeah. It was okay. I wasn't freaking on it or anything, but I did like it. Anyway, one day Len said that we should go up to a place he knows and shoot outside. He was going to set up some targets and we could do a combat thing. The Patriots did that a lot. I wasn't particularly interested in it and neither was Carla, but Len pushed it and we decided to go. We took his mother's Jeep. Carla didn't mind shooting, but she was more into just hanging out, listening to jams, talking. She liked to smoke, too.

RE: Marijuana?

CP: Right.

[There is a significant pause here.]

52

RE: So you went to this place to shoot. . . .

CP: Curry Woods. We got there and sat in the car for a while and just talked. Then he brought out this map he had drawn up. He could draw pretty well. From where he had parked the car, we could follow the map and pick out the different trees and a small hill. He said he had put the targets out the night before. There were six of them. The object was to shoot all six and get out of there before someone heard the noise of the guns and came to look into it. It was supposed to be a test for Carla and me, I knew, because Len had put the targets out. Anyway, we found them and shot five of them. They were orange bags hanging from trees, and right away I had a bad feeling about it. I asked Len what was in the bags and he said not to worry about it, that they were just targets. Carla must have had a bad feeling about it too. When we found the last target, she went right up to it. She must have been ten, no, five feet away and Len shot it. She didn't even stop. She took it down and opened it up. Then she came back and walked right past us to the car.

Turtles. The kind you buy in the pet store. There were four turtles in the bag.

Carla was pissed. She said Len should have told us what was in the bags. He kept saying that he had told us. "Targets." That's what he said. We started back

53

toward town and nobody said anything. That was it.

RE: How did you feel?

CP: Not great, for sure. Then Carla got on my case. She said I was worse than Len, because Len was just weird but I was like a lackey because I went along with it without saying anything. Then I got mad and told her that she had known something was in the bag. That we all knew. Then we got into a big fight. Not physical, just shouting. A lot of cursing. That kind of thing.

RE: You said we all "knew." What did you all know?

CP: That something was in the bag. It was the mysterious way that Len took us out there. The bags were just hanging from the trees and they were bright so you couldn't miss them. He just wanted us to shoot them.

RE: Did that make you feel different toward Len?

CP: It did make me think that he might be a different kind of guy than I had thought.

RE: Wait a minute. Are you telling me that up to that point you didn't realize he was—how do you put it—different?

CP: Len was outside, but a lot of kids at Madison were outside. He had gone dark, and that wasn't any big thing. I was outside. Carla was outside. I could have given you a list of thirty or forty kids who were outside, and another list of kids who had gone dark.

RE: Define "outside" for me.

CP: Kids who didn't belong. Like me. One time I was sitting

54

on the side steps, the ones that lead to the Media Center, and I was watching the freshies getting on a bus. And there were a couple of them who I could tell were outside already.

RE: Who probably wouldn't fit in.

CP: Okay, so if you know what I mean about that, then you can see that Len's being outside didn't make a big difference. But shooting the turtles did make a difference. The turtles were alive. Or maybe just not telling us was what made it bad.

RE: Did you feel bad when Carla got on your case?

CP: Yes. Because I knew she was right. In a way I knew she was right.

RE: Did you ever confront Len about it? Did you ever tell him how you felt about the incident?

CP: I was going to, but he was so pissed at Carla. I mean he was furious, man. When he got really mad, he turned red and even stuttered when he talked. He was pounding the dashboard. He was really mad. I decided to wait until he was calmer. Then it got away.

RE: What got away? You weren't angry with him anymore?

CP: The moment got away. The moment to confront him about it.

RE: Did he get angry a lot?

CP: Yeah—that was all in the papers.

RE: As you can imagine, I've read a lot of material, but I

55

would like to hear it from you. As you were saying earlier, the newspapers want to put their own spin on things.

CP: And kids are making up stories left and right. It looks like if you put a microphone in front of a kid at Madison or point a camera at some kid, they become instant experts. Half the kids walking around in dark clothes now are just biting air.

RE: So why don't you tell me about Len's anger.

CP: He had a hard time dealing with it. He would get mad at people for just about anything. Once we went into The Short Stop—they just sold snacks, milk, and a few other grocery items. Len asked the clerk for a diet soda and the guy asked him why he wanted a diet soda, as thin as he was. That set Len off big-time. He wanted to come back that night and burn the place down. I think he did drive by and throw a rock at it or something.

RE: Why did that get him pissed?

CP: He was very self-conscious about his body. He would never take his shirt off or let you see his arms or legs. He didn't like fat people, but he was uptight about being skinny.

RE: But wearing black made him look thinner, didn't it?

CP: No, it made him look like a certain kind of person. You know, when you're outside, and I told you I think a lot of kids are outside, and then you shut the door—he always talked about shutting the door—

RE: What is shutting the door?

CP: You're outside, so you do something that shuts the door so people know you don't want to come back in. That's important. I mean, when there's a fat guy, for example, and he's outside, if he's fat and he dyes his hair blue, then everybody knows he doesn't want to fit in. Going dark told everybody that Len didn't want to get along.

RE: So he went back and threw a rock at the store. Did he always get back at people he didn't like?

CP: No, sometimes he just put them on his list. I think he meant to get back at them someday.

RE: Is that the list everybody was— I read in the paper that he had an "enemies list" and that he would tell people he was putting them on the list. Is this the one you're talking about?

CP: Yes.

RE: Did you ever see it?

CP: No.

RE: That's hard to believe.

CP: I never saw his enemies list. I know he had one—he talked about it all the time. But it could have even been in his head. The sheriff's department asked me about it a dozen times.

RE: Okay. Okay. When did the turtle incident happen?

CP: It was just before Easter.

RE: And you say that everything was smooth after that?

CP: Smooth? No, first his father got dissed big-time, which was a major thing. He told me his father was dealing with the people in his company, looking for a promotion. Len's family did okay, but they weren't moving anyplace. His father had this thing that was, like, he needed to show everybody what he could do. He always said that he could kill the average man in less than four seconds.

RE: Four seconds?

CP: Well, he's a big guy. I didn't think he could kill somebody in four seconds, but he had Ranger training and all. And he's really into guns. I told you that before. He also drank a lot and that used up a lot of money, so they were always on the edge. Anyway, sometimes if he forgot something at home, he would have Len and me bring it down to where he worked. So I had seen his job and it was cool. Interesting. He dispatched all of these trucks and they were, like, huge. Len said we should steal one, but I thought he was just kidding.

One day after school Len needed some money and asked his mother, and she said she didn't have any and he was pissed, and she said for him to go to his father at his job and get some. He didn't like asking his father for money, but he needed to have his prescription filled. He had two prescriptions.

RE: Do you know what drugs he was taking?

CP: It was the same drug, but he had two prescriptions at two different drugstores.

RE: Why would he have two prescriptions?

CP: So he'd always have enough to calm him down or mellow him out, whatever he needed.

RE: He abused the prescription.

CP: Whatever. So he needed money for them, and we went down to his father's job and his father was getting chewed out by his boss. I guess it was his boss, because he was all up in Len's father's face. I mean all up in his face. And that set Len off big-time. We were driving in his car, and he spun out and sped down the road so fast, I thought he was going to kill us for sure. We drove about a half hour, maybe forty minutes, and then we parked down from the school. He cried. He really cried.

RE: What got to him? I don't understand.

CP: I think he thought his father should have taken the guy out. He should have punched him out or something. Instead he was just standing there squirming. Maybe he thought his father was nerding out. I don't know.

RE: I got the impression he didn't get along with his father?

CP: They weren't tight, so it surprised me when Len got so upset, especially when he started to cry. He was really like sobbing and shaking.

RE: How did that make you feel?

CP: That's like an obvious question. You don't want to see

anybody crying like that. How do you *think* it would make me feel? It was like everything had fallen apart for him. What he said was that the world wasn't working anymore. I mean, he used some pretty foul language, but that's what he said.

RE: Do you remember exactly what he said?

CP: It doesn't make a difference. He was pretty upset, and that was the thing.

RE: I still would like to hear the exact words, if you can remember them.

[There is a significant pause here.]

RE: Cameron, are you okay?

CP: Am I?

RE: You still really admire Len, is that right?

CP: At first, right after the incident, I didn't. And I don't think I admire him now. But the more I think about him, the more I talk about him, the more I understand him. And when you understand somebody, that changes your relationship with them. I don't know if you can get next to that, but that's the way it goes. At least for me. Sometimes I think I don't want to understand Len, because I don't want to like him, or admire him. But I think you can reach a point that you don't like a person but you're close to him because you're into his head. That's what happened, or that's what's happening with the way I feel about Len.

RE: How did you feel about his father that day?

CP: I think if I was as tough as he was, I wouldn't let anybody talk to me that way.

RE: Do you think that maybe he wasn't as tough as he talked? That maybe all the guns and the talk of Ranger training was because he wasn't that tough after all?

CP: Do you know that?

RE: No, I don't, but I wanted to know what you felt about it.

CP: You don't know it, and I don't know it either.

RE: Are you offended? Did I say something to make you angry?

CP: No, but I don't want to start a lot of guessing games, which is what so many people are doing. The newspaper people do that all the time. They're making the news.

RE: This is getting close, timewise, to the date of the incident. But during the weeks just prior to April twenty-second, you were having mixed feelings about Len, isn't that right?

CP: We weren't smooth. He started on Carla's case. He thought she had sniped him.

RE: Sniped him?

CP: He thought she had done him dirty. He said he trusted her, but then she turned against him because of the turtle incident. Then he turned on her. He said she was on his enemies list, and I didn't think she should have been. He got back at her, and that really messed me around.

RE: What did he do to get back at her?

CP: She had been in therapy. I didn't know that, but Len did. He got her therapy records. He broke in at night and went through the files until he found her records. He said they had all the computers locked up and all the telephone equipment locked but not the files. What he found out was that she had been molested. And he put it on the Circuit. The Circuit's an e-mail chain at the school that mostly the snobs and jocks use. It's like an open putdown forum. It wasn't signed and at first nobody believed it. But when Carla started crying, all the jocks started to run with it. Carla tried to tough it out, but they stayed on her. The jocks stayed on her, and some of the girls.

RE: That was an unbelievably cruel thing to do.

CP: Yes, it was.

RE: And you knew he had done it?

CP: I thought he had, and then when it was all over the school, he told me.

RE: And then what happened?

CP: We didn't speak for two or three days. I was the only one who knew who had put the stuff about Carla on the Circuit, and he told me he was sorry and that he shouldn't have done it.

RE: But you still liked him in a way?

CP: Maybe I didn't like him. I don't know. I'm not sure, I

guess. I think I was just safe with Len. Not physically, but he was like the one guy I knew who really understood how I felt just about all the time and didn't try to punk me out or dump on me.

RE: The one guy you could tell how you felt?

CP: No, Len understood people. He could be around somebody for two minutes and know who they were. He could really tell about people.

RE: Do you think he understood who his father was?

CP: I don't know.

RE: How did you get back to talking?

CP: I had had a fight with my father. Another fight. Every time we got into it, he would bring up the time I quit the basketball team. It was like he couldn't get over it, like I had done something to him personally. We got into it when he asked me if I wanted to go to some club and play tennis with him and I said no. I knew what it would be about, some big competition thing. Then he went on about how I should pay more attention to sports and how a lot of big business deals were made in locker rooms. Then it was right back to how I had quit in basketball and how I was just a quitter. It was like he was beating me up without hitting me.

RE: The same as they did in school.

CP: Yeah. Then he told me to get the basketball and we'd play one-on-one. I knew he would hack me to death and then put me down for not being tougher, you know. I said no, and he asked me why he should pay for my college when I wasn't even trying to get an athletic scholarship to help. He went on about how many hours he was working to support my—

[Here there is a significant pause.]

RE: To support your—

CP: To support my "sorry ass." Then he said I should play him one-on-one, and that if I beat him he would pay for my college. I was so mad. I got the ball and we went to the court, the one over at Lincoln Park. He's good, but in a fair game I think I would have a chance. But he kept beating on me and beating on me. Then he elbowed me in the chest, really hard. I wanted to do the same thing to him but I just couldn't. I just couldn't. I ended up with a bruise on my face.

RE: And on your ego.

CP: Yeah, I felt bad. Real bad. I don't want that part on tape, if it's okay with you. I just don't want to deal with it.

RE: What happened then?

CP: I stayed home for two days, and then one day Len came by. My face was still messed up and I told him what had happened. That's when he told me about his plan. He said he needed to break the silence. I asked him what that meant, and he said that everybody was agreeing to keep quiet about the violence in school. Mr. Washington, the teachers, the coaches, everybody wanted it kept quiet because it was easier to deal with that way. Just let some kids suffer and hope they make out all right. Len said he was going to break a hole in the wall of silence so big it couldn't be fixed. He asked me if I wanted to be part of it.

[Here there is a significant pause.]

RE: And what did you say?

CP: At first I told him that I didn't know. Then, when he said he was just going to write on the walls—he was going to write "Stop the Violence" in blood . . .

[Here there is a significant pause, followed by the sound of crying.]

Madison High School Incident Analysis
Report II—Interview with Cameron Porter
Submitted by Special Agent Victoria Lash,
Federal Bureau of Investigation
Threat Assessment Analyst

Mr. Porter is an African American, 5'11", with short hair and regular features. All pertinent records are on file.

Note to transcriber: Please do not note pauses.

Victoria Lash: Mr. Porter, please tell me as much
    as you can about Ordo Saggitae.

Cameron Porter: It was just a made-up group.
    Nothing special. Len thought it would be funny
    to name a group after something his
    grandmother had been in when she was going
    to college.

VL: How many members did it have?

CP: Five at the most. But they were only members
    in the sense that we all sat around one day and
    said, "Hey, let's start a club and everyone here
    is in it." There weren't any regular meetings.
    Even when me, Len, and Carla got together, it
    wasn't what you would call a regular meeting.

VL: There's a club on the school campus called
    Ordo Saggitae now. From what we can assess,
    there're about thirty to forty members.

CP: That was all made up after the newspapers
    started making a big deal of it. I guess kids
    wanted to belong to something.

VL: Is that what you wanted? To belong to
    something?

CP: I guess so. Yes.

VL: Why didn't you join the Boy Scouts?

CP: That is so lame. That is really so lame.

VL: What you wanted was to join a club or

organization that had some special
significance to you. Isn't that right?

CP: Yes.

VL: And so you, along with Len and Carla, as I
understand it, formed Ordo Saggitae.

CP: It was mostly Len's idea.

VL: So you had this club and you were connected
with another club—the Patriots. Is that right?

CP: You're making too much of it. The way you're
putting it is like there was this very formal club,
and then there's a link between us and another
club and we all believed in something special
or sinister. It's not like that at all.

VL: Did you and Len shoot at the Patriots' range?

CP: Yes.

VL: And at least on one occasion you signed
yourself onto the range as Ordo Saggitae. Is
that right?

CP: I don't remember that, but it could be.

VL: Well, let me ask you, Cameron. You're known to
be quite smart. What do you make of this
nonformal or informal connection? When I
spoke to the members of the Patriots, they
called themselves a loose-knit organization of
people—they should have said men—who were
more or less like-minded. They viewed

themselves as slightly out of the mainstream. They liked to shoot and they had an array of weapons. You're picturing Ordo Saggitae in the same way. What do you make of that?

CP: I don't want to be disrespectful—

VL: You won't be.

CP: There are a lot of organizations that are loose like that. I mean, if you go around the school and find out how many groups there are—it's all about kids following their flavors or getting a particular kind of interest going. It's not diabolical or anything close to it.

VL: But the group still existed, didn't it? And when you met on the twenty-second of April, was that an organized meeting of the Order of the Arrow?

CP: By the time the incident occurred, we weren't even talking about Ordo Saggitae.

VL: When you say "the incident," are you referring to the shootings?

CP: Yeah.

VL: You're referring to murder as an "incident"?

CP: Yes.

VL: You shot in the woods at one time. Tell me about that.

CP: Len set up these targets. They turned out to be

turtles in small orange bags. We shot at the bags and then found out there were turtles in them. The whole thing was over in minutes. No big deal except that I didn't want to kill the turtles. Carla didn't want to kill the turtles.

VL: Just a few minutes of killing, and it wasn't really a big deal. Is that what you're saying?

CP: I didn't know it was—that we were killing anything when we were shooting.

VL: Was there another time you shot with Len? I saw one report that mentioned a handgun being fired behind a supermarket.

CP: He had—his father had a Ruger, a really nice gun. We went behind the supermarket one night and fired it.

VL: What did you shoot at?

CP: The Dumpster. There was a poster on the Dumpster with some rock group on it and we shot at that.

VL: What was in the Dumpster?

CP: Nothing.

VL: Did you look?

CP: No.

VL: So you just sort of go along with the program, is that what you're saying?

CP: I didn't think there would be anything alive in

the Dumpster. It was just a garbage Dumpster. There wasn't anything in it except garbage.

VL: You got along well with Len, didn't you?

CP: Yes.

VL: Who was bigger?

CP: I'm a little taller.

VL: Stronger?

CP: Probably.

VL: You ever wrestle with him? Or box?

CP: No, he didn't like anything physical. Sometimes he watched sports, but he didn't play.

VL: What did he think of you?

CP: We got along.

VL: Cameron, it doesn't make sense for you to just "get along" with somebody and do the kinds of things you and Len did together. Does it?

CP: Len liked me. We were easy with each other. I was, like, straight up with him, and he was straight up with me.

VL: Which means?

CP: I didn't game him or anything.

VL: At the Patriots' range, you shot at targets. I understand there was a politically incorrect target at the range. That didn't bother you, though?

CP: It bothered me. I knew that some of the people

at the range were probably racists. I knew that. They talked about being patriots and loving their country, but I knew that what they meant was loving the images they had of their country. I knew that.

VL: But you were still willing to go along with it even though the racism was directed at your people. I guess you felt that if you didn't think about it too hard, it would be all right?

CP: I don't know what I thought.

VL: Well, let me ask you. Did you think? Did you go home and say to yourself, "Hey, they were shooting at an image of Martin Luther King out there"? Did you ask yourself if that was the right thing to do?

CP: I knew it wasn't, so I just sort of put it out of my mind.

VL: That's because you enjoyed shooting at their range?

CP: I guess so.

VL: And what about Len? Did he come over to you and say something to the effect of "Hey, buddy, sorry about the racism"?

CP: He laughed it off. That's the way he handled things sometimes. He would just laugh it off like it didn't matter.

VL: Or as if you and he were above the racists?

CP: At least apart from them.

VL: You set yourselves apart from the racists, and apart from most people. Isn't that right?

CP: We were apart, but I don't think we set ourselves apart. Most of the time, even before I started hanging with Len, I felt apart.

VL: You knew about Len breaking into the clinic's offices and stealing records. Is that right?

CP: He told me.

VL: But there's no way of really knowing if you helped him or not, is there?

CP: I didn't help him.

VL: He wanted the records and he found a way of getting them. He abused prescription drugs, and he found a way of getting them. Did you know about the double prescriptions?

CP: Yes.

VL: And did you ever lie in your bed and say, "Hey, you know what? My friend is doing something that could be dangerous to his health—maybe I should tell someone"? Did you ever think that?

CP: Honestly? No. I knew Len was doing things, and that some of them were illegal, or even dangerous. But if I was going to start ratting him out, I would have rather just stayed away from him. A lot of kids are doing things that aren't legal. I don't rat them out.

VL: No matter how dangerous?

CP: If it got dangerous enough, I guess I would.

VL: So if he did something like acquire automatic weapons, you would . . . what would you do?

CP: I didn't do anything.

VL: Len took Carla's records from the clinic. You said in your last interview that you thought that was wrong. Did you mean that?

CP: Yes, I did.

VL: What do you think of Carla?

CP: I like her.

VL: You ever think about hitting on her?

CP: Not in that way.

VL: Look, you're both young. You're male, and she's female. Carla's good-looking and she's willing to hang out. You're telling me you never thought you would like to make out with her?

CP: I thought about it.

VL: Did you ever kiss her?

CP: No—once.

VL: Once.

CP: She was down after the thing in school and I kissed her once. I didn't push it or anything.

VL: Did you feel her up?

CP: No!

VL: It was relatively easy for Len to get the drugs he wanted and to get Carla's records. He also got weapons. How did he get them?

CP: I only know about two pieces he had. He bought an old AR-18 from one guy and the Galil after that.

VL: I don't remember seeing anything about the AR-18 in the records. When did he buy it?

CP: He bought that a while ago, before Christmas maybe, or just after.

VL: Where did he get it?

CP: At a gun show. Not from one of the regular dealers. You know, you go to a gun show and there's always private deals going on.

VL: What was the difference between the two pieces?

CP: The AR-18 shot more rounds per minute. The other gun looked cooler, but they both used the same ammo.

VL: And the police recovered a Kalashnikov. That's the coolest of them all?

CP: The barrel doesn't go up much on automatic. You can stay on target easier.

VL: You know that from comparing them on a range?

CP: I read it in a magazine. Len had lots of gun magazines. I had gun magazines too. We read them and survivor-type magazines. It's got to be in your reports.

VL: Going back to Ordo Saggitae. There was some mention that no Jews were allowed in the organization. Is that correct?

CP: No, not exactly. Len would get angry at people, or at some event, and then he would go off on it. He would get, like, furious, and then that person or that group would be on his list. I don't think he was against any group. But something would come up and he would explode and that's what happened with the Jewish thing. He never mentioned Jews until one day a teacher made some remark about his not being the leading-man type. They were casting a school play and somebody said that Len should play the lead. It was sort of a joke and he didn't like it. Then when she sort of knocked it off with the thing about him not being the leading-man type, he went off. The teacher was Jewish. But I don't think Len had it in for Jews.

VL: It sounds to me as if he had a lot of free-floating hate that he spread around pretty liberally.

CP: I guess.

VL: His enemies list was never found. Do you have an enemies list?

CP: No.

VL: You're just all sweetness and light, aren't you?

CP: Is that what you're supposed to do? Mess over me?

VL: Well, what I'm trying to figure out, Cameron, is who led whom. Did Len drag you to the shooting range, or did you use him to get to shoot? Was he leading you, or were you behind him pushing him forward? What do you think?

CP: I don't—we had a relationship—we were friends. I don't think that I was just a follower and I know I wasn't pushing him into anything that he didn't want to do. Not really.

VL: Not really. He didn't really hate Jews. He didn't really hate anybody. He just got very mad at people and claimed he hated them. So tell me, how did he "not really" threaten to shoot this teacher?

CP: He said he would shoot her, but he kept saying that and . . . I didn't think he meant it.

VL: But there were a number of threats against people, and you were aware of them?

CP: And there were a number of threats against us, too. And a number of threats against Len. Jocks saying they were going to beat him up. Saying they were going to make him lick their shoes. And not only threats. He was hit. He was smacked around and everyone knew it.

VL: And you were pushed around. So I can imagine how you felt when you were being bullied. Did you feel the same way when you saw Len being bullied?

CP: The same way? Yeah, I guess. Actually, when I saw him being pushed around, saw guys getting into his face and putting him down, it was almost the same as if it was me. It was like I was recognizing something in Len that was the same as it was in me. Only when things like that happened, he got madder than me.

VL: How do you feel if somebody is pushing you around? You don't get mad?

CP: Mostly I get disappointed.

VL: Disappointed that someone is acting badly?

CP: Disappointed that I don't do something about it. Disappointed in the way I feel inside.

VL: And when was it decided to do something about all of these incidents? . . . Cameron?

CP: We were always thinking about doing

something. We went to the principal once.

VL: Cameron, you're hesitating with your answers. When I ask you a question, I want an answer. I don't want these long pauses. You've had enough time to consider these things, haven't you?

CP: You don't want me to think about what I'm going to say?

VL: You've been over this enough times to know the answers. You gave interviews—no, you didn't give interviews to the papers—but you did have the interview with Dr. Ewings, you had intensive questioning from the police right after the murder, and you've certainly had sufficient time to think this thing through. Tell me what happened when you spoke to the principal.

CP: He said, more or less, that dealing with other teenagers was part of the growing-up process. It was something I had to learn how to do. It was more or less the same thing that my father was saying, only he said it in a different way.

VL: How did your father say it?

CP: He said I needed to toughen up, grow up. Stuff like that. Then he fell into his usual rap about how he was tough inside and how that helped him in business.

VL: You get an allowance?

CP: Fifty dollars a week. It's not really an allowance. It's what I get to draw down without a lot of questions.

VL: Draw down?

CP: I take it out of the ATM. My parents have an account at First Savings.

VL: And what do you have to do for the fifty dollars?

CP: Nothing, really.

VL: That should toughen you up, shouldn't it?

CP: Whatever.

VL: How much is in the account all together? I don't need an exact figure, just an estimate.

CP: Why?

VL: I don't have to tell you why. You're not my equal here, Cameron. I thought we had established that. How much is in the account?

CP: They usually keep about six to eight thousand in it. It's an interest account. I think they get something like two percent. Not much.

VL: Not much interest or not much money in the account?

CP: Not much interest.

VL: Do you have an account of your own? And if

you do, give me as close an estimate as you can of how much money you have in it.

CP: About two thousand dollars. Less than that, somewhere around fifteen hundred.

VL: Did you have more or less before the incident?

CP: About the same. Maybe a little more. I don't remember.

VL: I read in your interview with Dr. Ewings that your mother was having a pool built into the house. Do you know how much that cost?

CP: No.

VL: I don't believe you. Your parents are very money conscious. Money-conscious people talk prices.

CP: They worked hard for their money. Nobody gave it to them. They weren't taking anything from the government. They make more than most people. They make more than you do. Does that bother you?

VL: No, it doesn't. I'm white and you're black; does that bother you?

CP: No, it doesn't.

VL: Good. Now, how much did the pool cost?

CP: I don't really remember. I didn't really like to hear—to discuss how much things cost.

VL: Why didn't you want to hear about them? . . .

Cameron? . . . Here we go with our significant pauses again. I'm asking you questions, Cameron, and I want you to answer them. You owe this community answers to these questions, and the best answers that you can come up with, young man. Now, why didn't you want to hear about what things cost?

CP: I think I wanted something else. I wanted to talk about other things. That's all they seemed to want to talk about. On my birthday my father . . .

VL: On your birthday your father *what*?

CP: He took me out to dinner, me and my mother. It was okay, and when it was time to pay the check, he just signed it and we started to walk out. I thought the waiter would stop us or something. But we just got up and walked out. In the car he told me he had arranged for a standing account at the restaurant. That was my birthday present. I could take my friends to that restaurant.

VL: So you could display your financial status?

CP: Yeah.

VL: And you didn't like it?

CP: I knew it was supposed to be something special, but it was like getting good grades in school or a good SAT score. It would just make me stand out.

VL: Did you ever take any of your friends to the restaurant?

CP: No.

VL: You didn't mention many friends other than Len and Carla. Do you have trouble getting along with people?

CP: I don't mean to pause all the time, but I don't know all the answers. As far as getting along with people, it depends on a lot of things. When I was in the lower grades, I got along better. But if you run into one or two guys who need to find somebody to put down, and they happen to pick you, then you've got a problem. It's cool to have friends, but they don't count as much—they count, but they don't seem as important in your life as the people who are putting you down.

VL: And someone like Len—someone who "gets mad" and who has access to guns, he can balance things out, can't he?

CP: I don't know if I would say that.

VL: You're suggesting that your father doesn't see things the way you do. You spend much time with him?

CP: He travels a lot.

VL: How much?

CP: Sometimes he's away half the month. He stays in touch by phone. He's even got a videocam he hooks up to his laptop so you can see him when he calls.

VL: And your mother works how many hours a day? You said she worked hard.

CP: She puts in a lot of hours—she's home by eight, usually. All the time by eight.

VL: So more or less you're on your own.

CP: No, they're there when I need them to be there. And whatever they're doing, they're building a life for the whole family.

VL: Did you ever wish you had a brother or sister?

CP: Not really.

VL: The two rifles that Len bought. How much did he pay for them?

CP: I don't know. I wasn't with him when he bought them and he didn't tell me.

VL: No, you did buy one rifle with him. That was the Israeli rifle, the Galil, and some ammunition. That was in the police record. How much did that cost?

CP: Around four or five hundred dollars.

VL: That was a good buy. Who negotiated that buy?

CP: Len.

VL: And you were in the kitchen washing the teacups?

CP: What does that mean?

VL: It means that you paint a very precious picture of yourself, Cameron. Very precious and very careful.

CP: I'm not painting—

VL: Think back on the time you were at the gun show. How did that make you feel?

CP: I liked it—it was okay. I liked looking at all the stuff.

VL: And you like talking about "all the stuff" and reading about "all the stuff." How does that make you feel?

CP: You mean, does it give me a sense of power or something?

VL: You tell me.

CP: No, it doesn't. There's macho stuff going around the shows, but I wasn't turning into a gun freak or anything.

VL: How did you meet the man who sold you the Galil?

CP: He was one of the younger guys at the Patriots range.

VL: He sold you one of his rifles?

CP: They're always buying and selling weapons. They're not like target shooters. They're more like military people—soldiers, I guess.

VL: What's the difference between military people and target shooters?

CP: I'm not sure, but I think there are people who like to shoot. It's like a hobby or a sport. They get good weapons and they talk about taking care of them, maybe loading—you know, how many grains to load for a certain velocity, that kind of thing.

VL: You ever do your own loading?

CP: No.

VL: Go on.

CP: Other guys go more for power weapons. They buy other stuff as well as guns—knives, combat gear. When we went to the range, we either used Len's father's weapons or borrowed weapons from the range house. Len wanted his own piece, so he looked around and then he spotted this guy. He said he didn't have any extra weapons but he knew somebody who was selling, and so that's what happened.

VL: So that's what happened. If I gave you one thousand five hundred dollars right now, how would you go about getting an AK-47, collapsible stock, with a telescopic sight, leather combat sling, and two clips of ammo?

CP: Probably go to a gun show. Look around for guys wearing combat gear.

VL: They come to the show in camouflage suits?

CP: No, but they often wear something. Maybe fatigue pants, or a military patch. Something. They hang around the sellers with the power weapons and talk a lot. You can hear them talk and they'll usually say what they have, what kinds of weapons they have. The other stuff, the sight and sling, you can buy anywhere.

VL: So if you're bullied, if you're pushed around by a bigger guy or a tougher guy, you can always get an equalizer?

CP: I don't think—we weren't thinking of the guns as "equalizers."

VL: But it's not a stretch, is it?

CP: No.

VL: What did your parents think of you shooting?

CP: They thought it was like a social club. I didn't discuss it with them much.

VL: Whose idea was it to get Carla to the range? Usually that's not a girl's activity unless some guy pushes her into it.

CP: I don't remember. Probably Len, because his

dad belonged to the club.

VL: So we have this little group of three people. You, Len, and Carla. You hang out together, you shoot together, and you forgive one another your little transgressions. But according to you, Len was the head of this little group even though you were the biggest, and by all accounts the one with the most money, and the best athlete. So how did Len become the leader?

CP: I didn't see him as a leader so much as just a guy I felt comfortable with. I didn't have a lot of friends, and when I started hanging out with him, it was easy to keep doing it.

VL: What religion are you?

CP: Presbyterian.

VL: You go to church on a regular basis?

CP: Not really.

VL: So you don't—let's put it this way—do you think of yourself as religious?

CP: In a way. I wouldn't say very religious.

VL: You're black. Do you belong to any—do you prefer "African American"?

CP: I don't care.

VL: Do you belong to any African American organizations?

CP: Which organizations?

VL: I'll take that as a no. I read that you were good enough to play on the school basketball team but stopped playing. You didn't like the team?

CP: I'm an okay player, not that good. Mostly I like to play, but I'm not heavy into competition. It's not like I just have to win. I was on the bubble, then I got cut, then my father pulled some kind of strings to get me on the team.

VL: Did your father's "pulling strings" mess it up for you?

CP: In a way.

VL: Cameron, I'm getting mixed signals here. On one hand I'm getting the idea that you and Len were being bullied or pushed away from the mainstream. On the other hand I'm seeing you as a person who deliberately moves away from groups. You don't identify yourself as a religious person and so you don't attend a church, which is a group you could belong to if you wanted. You don't seem to have any strong ethnic feelings. I know what you said about your father's attitude toward your playing on the basketball team, but I can't help noticing that this is another instance of your moving away from another group.

CP: I didn't—you know, it's not like I—

VL: Are you okay?

CP: Yeah.

VL: You were talking about belonging to groups . . . ?

CP: It's not like I didn't *want* to be in a group, or have friends. I just sort of looked for people who thought I was okay.

VL: Like Len.

CP: Like Len.

VL: Len was going to the same clinic as Carla. What was he doing at the clinic? Did he discuss that with you?

CP: He was talking to a psychiatrist. He said it was a butterfly game. The psychiatrist had him pinned down and was trying to stick a label under his body. That was the way Len talked a lot.

VL: If you were to stick a label under his body, what would it be?

CP: Sometimes he was mixed up. He had a few problems.

VL: Besides the problems of being bullied in school, what problems did he have? Were they physical? Mental? Sexual?

CP: I don't think they were that bad. Lots of people have problems, but some people can handle them better than others. I don't think he had any sexual problems. He was interested in Carla, but they weren't, you know, doing anything.

VL: He told you that?

CP: Yeah.

VL: You were involved—when I say "you," I mean Cameron the Presbyterian—with Len in a church-vandalizing incident. Tell me about that.

CP: It wasn't against the church, or against God. It was like we were there, and it was a symbolic thing. It was stupid.

VL: And indecent?

CP: Yeah. But we didn't do anything sacrilegious. We put some paint on the walls.

VL: Besides the message that "God doesn't live here" and the sign you wrote about Jesus, there was also the number eighty-eight painted on the wall. What does that mean?

CP: I think Len just made up a number to see what they would think it meant.

VL: And what did "they" think it meant?

CP: They thought that it was like 187, which stands for homicide. But it was just a made-up number.

VL: Except that you and I know it stands for "Heil,

Hitler," don't we? Don't we know that, Cameron?

CP: I didn't know that at the time. A lot of the things that I know now I didn't know when it was happening. I saw Len writing on the wall. I was a little nervous—a lot nervous—and I wanted to get out of there, so I didn't get into any discussions about it.

VL: So eventually you had to go down to the police station with your parents. You had a lawyer and Len had a lawyer. And your father and Len's father agreed to pay for the damage. The church wanted to press charges, but your lawyer said that both of you were going through difficult times and came up with a sob story. Is that right?

CP: Yeah.

VL: And so you got out of the whole incident and a judge assigned both of you to have continuing psychological evaluations. That's confidential information, so I couldn't get it in my role as an evaluator. What came out of that? Did you consider it a game the way that Len did?

CP: No. I liked talking to the counselor. I think it helped me to think over some things.

VL: By the way, some kids just avoid bullies. They

walk home a different way, they associate with
a different crowd. Why didn't you and Len do
that? Did that ever occur to you?

CP: Yes, it did, but . . . sometimes you try to figure
out who you are. Who you really are inside. And
you think that maybe you're okay, or close to
being okay, and maybe things will change down
the line. But then somebody else comes up to
you and they say—the words that come out of
their mouth may be like—"Hey, faggot, give me
a dollar." Or "Hey Cameron, what are you
looking at? Look someplace else or I'll beat the
crap out of you"—and what they're really
saying is that you're nothing. That's what
they're saying. And then when they say that,
they look at you and wait for your answer. And
when you put your head down and walk away,
or when you look away when they tell you to,
then you're saying the same thing, that you're
nothing. And so maybe you daydream about
doing something. Or maybe you imagine what
you would say if you only could get the nerve
up to do it. But deep inside, you know that
whoever gets up in your face gets there
because he knows you're nothing, and he
knows that you know it too.

VL: And if you find somebody, like Len, who has
the nerve to do something, you close your eyes
and follow him, even if he's as wrong as the
bully?

CP: You don't close your eyes.

VL: So with your eyes wide open, how much of this
did you see coming?

CP: I didn't think things would turn out the way
they did. I really didn't.

VL: Among Len's rather cryptic notes was what
looked to be a quote from Robert Frost, or a
Robert Frost–like quote. He said, "The road not
taken needs to be destroyed." Any idea what
that means?

CP: No.

VL: Len's notes are almost like a secret code. Did
he speak that way?

CP: Not really. He was pretty clear.

VL: He had been thinking about joining the Army.
Have you ever considered joining the Army?
Any branch of the military?

CP: Not really.

VL: If you were drafted, would you go?

CP: I haven't thought about it, but I think I would.

VL: I asked that question because I'm trying to
figure out if any of you, Len, Carla, or you, had

anything in your lives that you truly loved. Do you love your country?

CP: I guess so.

VL: Your values aren't very clear, are they?

CP: They're clearer now than they were.

VL: You had a run-in with your father and you made a big deal of that. There was a basketball game—he pushed you. You didn't like it. You pushed him back. You got physical with him and he got physical with you. You couldn't cope in a situation most guys could have handled. Do you think there's a problem with your coping skills?

CP: How do you know what most guys can handle? You think guys can handle things just because they don't get into trouble?

VL: That's one clue.

CP: A lot of guys my age aren't doing that well in the real world. And the same people who say guys ought to deal with their emotions and deal with things bothering them turn around and talk about how "most guys can handle things."

VL: Do you think you would handle things differently now?

CP: I have to say yes, but—and I've been thinking

about it—I don't know how I would handle
things differently. I know I'm so sorry that
things turned out the way they did. I just feel
terrible about it.

VL: Cameron, do you consider yourself a threat to
society?

CP: No. No, I don't.

VL: Did you consider yourself a threat to society
when you woke up on the morning of April
twenty-second?

CP: No, I didn't.

VL: I'm sorry, I didn't hear you.

CP: No, I didn't.

VL: What have you been doing since then?

CP: I've been working at the mall. Going to school
at night. I'm thinking about going away to
school next fall.

VL: Back to the good life?

CP: That's not how I see it.

VL: Cameron, the purpose of these interviews is to
find ways of avoiding future occurrences of
this type. We don't want any more young people
lying dead between the school buses. How
would you go about preventing it from
happening?

CP: I don't know how this happened. I don't know

how to prevent it from happening again. I just know I wish I could take it all back somehow. I don't know if you believe that, but it's true.

VL: What I believe, Cameron, is that you would like to take back the events of that April morning, but I'm not sure that you want to take back the events that led to that morning. I'm not even sure that you would recognize them if they came up again. Thank you for your time.

Madison High School Incident Analysis
Report III—Interview with Carla Evans
Submitted by Dr. Franklyn Bonner,
Spectrum Group, Threat Assessment Specialists

Carla Evans is now eighteen years of age. She was a senior at Madison High School at the time of the event that is the background subject of this report. Her public-school records indicate that Miss Evans moved to Harrison County from Saginaw, Michigan, and has been a county resident for two years. Her Saginaw record indicates some emotional problems and the use of prescription drugs during her middle-school years, and other medications, including some for asthma, subsequent to that period.

Her physical presentation is one of "rebellion." She is Caucasian, somewhat tall, and of average weight. There are streaks of blue dye in her brown hair and an overuse of makeup, including heavily drawn eyebrows that meet. She has her ears pierced in several spots and wears silver studs in lieu of conventional earrings. Her lipstick is multicolored, but applied with some care.

Carla's grades are in the low average range, and it is doubtful that she will go on to higher learning. She is currently working as a waitress at the V.I.P. Diner.

The interview was videotaped by an unmanned camera directed toward Carla. The overall impression is of a reasonably attractive young woman who, quite possibly, would be a standout with more care given to her personal appearance. Her dress is generally sloppy, with baggy woolen stockings that don't color match and a long, almost Victorian period skirt over which she wears a man's dress shirt. She wears a black lace glove on her left hand. She is punctual to the interview. She sits with her legs apart, her head to one side, and a slight smile on her face.

Franklyn Bonner: Carla, you've signed the Miranda statement and you do understand that we're here to further the investigation into possible future threats to students and other personnel in Harrison County?

Carla Evans: Yes.

FB: Carla, my name is Franklyn Bonner. I'm a psychologist and the president of a company whose job it is to analyze events and make predictions about the probability of similar events. To begin this interview, could you tell me something about your home life? I understand you live with a foster family?

CE: Right.

FB: Why do you live with this family?

CE: My folks split when we lived in Saginaw. I was living with my mom at first, but then she wasn't cutting it and I had to go live with my dad in his creepy trailer. I had some problems there and so I moved here and lived with an aunt for a while. Then I wasn't going to school on a regular basis, so they put me with a foster family. Case closed.

FB: What was your relationship with your mother? Did you get along with her?

CE: Yeah, we're a lot alike, more like sisters than anything else. But she doesn't have a lot of confidence in herself. After my dad left, she had a few boyfriends that messed over her and she really started to lose it. She didn't need me around causing trouble.

FB: What kind of trouble did you cause?

CE: Just being around, mostly. She could hardly take care of herself.

FB: Which means?

CE: I had to run things half the time because she couldn't. We got evicted from the place we were renting and she wanted to go back to Chicago—that's where she's from—to live with her brother and his wife. I didn't want to do that, so I moved in with my father.

FB: And what was that like?

CE: He's a loser.

FB: Can you elaborate on that?

CE: He didn't have anything going on. Just bouncing from job to job, blowing his money in bars, that sort of thing.

FB: You didn't like living with him?

CE: I was like his freaking maid half the time. Not because I wanted to be—I couldn't stand how dirty the place was. I tried to stay away from him. He didn't care. That's his thing, he would go around saying he didn't care. And you know what? It was true. All he cared about was his next beer.

FB: So it's fair to say that you didn't particularly like your father?

CE: No, it's not. I didn't like him or not like him. He was just there.

FB: How old were you at the time?

CE: I was twelve, almost thirteen. I had just got my period.

FB: You were running your house in Michigan when you were twelve?

CE: I'm pretty capable. I can deal with money.

FB: Why did you leave your father's house? His trailer?

CE: I had trouble that I'm not going to discuss.

FB: All right. You were a student at Madison for a relatively short time. Would you say that your tenure there was positive?

CE: Would I say what?

FB: Were you happy at Madison High School?

CE: It was okay.

FB: How did you first meet Leonard, and how did you first meet Cameron?

CE: I met Cameron first. He was really nice and I like black guys.

FB: Why is that?

CE: Because most black guys don't have a lot of baggage unless they're heavy into the "get whitey" thing. They have themselves, they have whatever they can do, but they don't have a lot of crap about who they're going to be or who you have to be. You meet most black guys and what you got in front of you is what you got. Cameron is a little different because his folks have money. They're into a serious show-and-tell thing. But he seemed nice and I wanted to meet him. When I met Len I told him I liked Cameron, because they were tight. Len and Cameron. But then Len came on to me really heavy. He could be really smooth—no, not smooth—sincere, he could be really sincere. He made you feel like he needed you. So I got interested in Len and I was still interested in Cameron, and since they were tight I was hanging with both of them. One thing I liked about Len was that he didn't try to crawl into my pants right away. Most boys want to get you into bed before they even know your name.

FB: Had you been to bed with other boys?

CE: Sort of.

FB: You can't "sort of" go to bed with a boy.

CE: Yeah you can. You can "sort of" do anything you want with a boy.

FB: Okay. I'll take your word for it. So what happened when you were friends with both of them?

CE: We started hanging. Len was real dark, and Cameron was getting there. I liked them both.

FB: Why did you like young men who were—how do you put it—dark?

CE: Because that's where I was. I wasn't exactly rolling with the band, man. I don't now. You might have noticed that. Len was outside, Cameron was outside, and I was, like, drifting in Geek City.

FB: Why do you think you were outside?

CE: Because that's where I wanted to be. I didn't want to go down no Yellow Brick Road or follow some bluebird to happiness. What I wanted was to walk my walk, talk my talk, and hear that lonesome whistle wail.

FB: That's very poetic.

CE: No it's not. It's bullshit. I wasn't getting it on and I was afraid to try because I didn't want to fall down. If you don't want to fall down, what you need to do is to stay outside because the ice is stone slippery inside.

FB: So when you found yourself "outside," you tried to establish that position as a coping strategy?

CE: You know, when you talk like that, I don't know what you're talking about, so I'm not going to answer.

FB: You were outside, and so you accepted that?

CE: I accepted it.

FB: I read that you actually shot guns on a range with Cameron and Leonard?

CE: I didn't go for it that tough. But when I got to it, I knew it was something I could do. You pull a trigger and hear a bang and then you go see how you made out. That's it. Over. Case closed. Nobody has to like you. Nobody forgets to call you the next day.

FB: Did you ever have sex with either Leonard or Cameron?

CE: You're investigating threats?

FB: I'm analyzing the possibility of future threats.

CE: So if I was having sex with Leonard, that makes me a threat?

FB: I just wanted to know how close you were with these two young men.

CE: Then sex doesn't have nothing to do with it. I wasn't having sex with either of them, but we were getting close in an emotional way.

FB: Describe Cameron and Leonard for me.

CE: Describe them? Well, Cameron is open. He's kind of gentle. He's built nice and cute in a young kind of way. He's not like a rapper or anything like that. If you get right in front of him and look at him hard—I mean if I got right in front of him and looked at him hard— he'd smile. I like that in a guy.

FB: And Leonard?

CE: He was cool. You always got the impression that there was something spinning around in his head. But he knew people, man. One day I was feeling lousy. The day had started out raggedy and was going downhill in a hurry. I was just going to finesse it out, but that wasn't working either. I'm sitting in the cafeteria and he comes over with a cup of tea and just puts it down and walks away. He just knew I needed some tea with lemon and no freaking conversation. He just put it down and walked away. That was Len.

FB: But eventually you had a falling out with Leonard?

CE: Yeah. He knew how to hurt, too. He was good at that.

FB: He posted some information about you on the Net. Can you tell me about that?

CE: It was personal information and I'm not going there. That's between me and my shrink.

FB: I need to understand the impact of all the incidents that led up to the tragic events of April twenty-second. We're trying to be as fair to everyone as we can. I understand, in your case, that there was some history of molestation?

CE: Excuse me. Do you speak English? Do you understand what I'm saying when I'm saying I'm not going there?

FB: Fine. Fine. Can you tell me what happened in the days leading up to April twenty-second?

CE: I was staying home. I had just, like, turned away from all the crap in school. My head was not so tight that I could really deal with everything going on. You know, people making remarks and what have you. All that's in the reports I gave to the police before.

FB: Okay, but can you go over the days just before the event?

CE: I talked to Cameron once or twice. He called my house and asked me if I was okay. He was mad at Len too. I didn't have a major conversation with him because I wasn't up to it. I was taking tranqs to mellow out.

FB: Tranquilizers? These were prescribed?

CE: Some were, some weren't. You can buy what you need at Madison. Then Len calls me and says he has to talk to me. So I'm like, "Hey, it's outrageous you even have my number in your brain. Get it out of

112

your brain before my phone stops working or something." He said he was sorry for the violence he laid on me.

FB: You had a physical confrontation with him?

CE: No, he was talking about putting my business in the street. He said he knew he shouldn't have done it and he was sorry for it.

FB: Did you believe that?

CE: Yes and no. Anybody who's going to tear your beard and show your pain is foul. I know that. But he sounded sincere and he nailed it down like violence against me, which it was. When I first went to the clinic and started talking about what had happened to me, I thought it was just like—what?—like something unfortunate. But the doctor there pointed out that it was about me being attacked. Even though there wasn't any hitting or fighting involved, I was still being attacked. That's when I got to know that violence was just as much about *what* was happening as it was how it happened. You know what I mean?

FB: Yes, I do. I do. Did you accept Leonard's apology?

CE: He didn't sound like he was gaming me or anything. I also have this thing about confrontations. It's like if I don't confront people about stuff, if I just get past it, I can put it out of my head. At least I thought I could put it out of my head. So when someone would mess with me and then said they were sorry, I would go for it. Not for them, but for me. But I was going to put a distance between us, between me and Len, and if I thought he was jerking my chain, I was going to jerk his.

FB: How was that supposed to work?

CE: I'm not a doctor, but I know some stuff too. One thing I knew was that you could get to Len. He always came off like he was pissed, but I knew you could hurt him too. I figured if he was jerking my chain, I would start making it with Cameron and that would get to him.

FB: That's rather convoluted, isn't it?

CE: No, it's not convoluted or revoluted. It's foul and I know it. But that's what's happening on this street. I mean, that's what we're talking about, isn't it? Foul stuff? That's why you're here, right?

FB: I guess so. So then what happened?

CE: So Len is steady laying this rap about how he's sorry about the pain he laid on me. He's rapping about how much garbage there is in the world and whatnot, and I'm listening and he's rapping and I'm listening and he's still rapping. Then he says he knows about this woman artist—Kira something—she did these paintings in blood. Blood. And what he was going to do was go to school and write "Stop the Violence" all over the school in his own blood.

FB: That's rather dramatic.

CE: Yeah, big-time. But I figured he was going to write it once at most or he would have to write it small because how much can you bleed? You've got about ten pints of blood in your body—I looked it up on the Internet—so you're not going to be writing no book. And I was supposed to be the one to fix the door.

FB: Fix the door?

CE: At night they lock all the doors and they don't unlock them until five minutes before school starts except for the front door. All the teachers and the maintenance crew and anybody who has to come in early have to come through that one door. I was supposed to go to the school early, bang on the back door, and tell whoever was there that I had to use the bathroom big-time. The girls' bathroom is on the first floor near that door. I was supposed to go in, then I go out of the same door and I push the little button on the door and it stays unlocked. I was going to bring some paint in, too, and leave it in the girls' bathroom for Len and Cameron. So I said okay, I'd do it. Then, as soon as school started, I was supposed to meet them in the library.

FB: You were going to do all this even though you were mad at him?

CE: One of the problems I have is that when things go wrong with me, I'm just looking for a way to get past it, you know, to make it go away. No matter what people do to me, I just want to get past it. It sucks, but it's where I go.

FB: So you were going to fix the door?

CE: I called Cameron. Cameron said that Len had told him the same thing and he wanted him to come along. Cameron said he wasn't sure, because it sounded like a big step and they might both get kicked out of school if they were caught.

FB: Cameron was worried about that?

CE: Yeah. But I wasn't because I wasn't planning to go back to school anyway.

FB: Did you think that painting on the walls was doing violence to the school?

CE: In a way. But it's like chaining yourself to a tree in order to save it. You know what I mean?

FB: It's a matter of opinion, but go on. Please.

CE: I got the paint. I asked for blood red and the guy gave me vermilion. Len called me at four that morning. He sounded a little weird, tired mostly. Or like he'd been smoking. He asked me if I was still coming and I told him yes. He said that he thought Cameron was backing out. He started slamming Cameron, and I told him to ease up because it was his show and that Cameron and I were just helping him. Then he eased off of Cameron and said he would see me at the school.

We have this old Chevy Cavalier that's like a hundred and nine years old and that's what I'm driving. The belt slips and it whistles and squeaks, so you can hear me coming down the street. So I got this paint, which was twenty-four dollars because it's art paint, and I start out to school. I'm supposed to get there at seven thirty and the first bell is eight oh five. But when I get to Felson's, the car is overheating, and by the time I get across the bridge it's cutting out. I have to sit and wait for the thing to cool off. I put water in the radiator and it's ready to boil over any minute. By the time I get to school, it's like ten to eight. I go to the door and I try it and it's already open. So I go in and look around. There's a maintenance guy reading a newspaper and drinking coffee. He doesn't see me and I slip into the stairwell. I start up the stairs, and just before I get to the third floor, I hear this commotion and all this freaking noise. When I get to the third floor, Cameron is there, all bug-eyed and wild looking. He's really freaked out. He has a gun. I'm like, "What's going on?" And then I see Len and he's got ammunition all wrapped around his body and I knew something big was going to happen. I was going to cool it, and I turn to Cameron to ask him what's going on, and then the whole window next to me like explodes. There's glass flying everywhere and noise and I'm half running and half being dragged by Cameron.

I bang my knee on the railing in the staircase and I'm falling down the stairs. I hear Len screaming something and I want to go back and help him because I think somebody's after him. But Cameron is still pulling me and I'm fighting him. Then I hear some more shots. Only they're louder than at the range and I'm scared. Cameron's yelling something but I don't know what because I'm too scared to think straight. Then he pushes me into a closet in the audiovisual room and closes the door. All I can remember after that is sitting in that closet crying and shaking. And oh yeah, I peed all over myself.

FB: Then what happened?

CE: Then I just sat there until a SWAT guy opened the door and took me out. They had Cameron handcuffed and they handcuffed me. That was it. The whole thing. I didn't know what else had happened until they told me that evening.

FB: Carla, what do you think of all this? If you were summing it up, what would you say?

CE: I've thought about it, naturally. The thing is that everybody is looking at what happened that day, but when you think about it, what happened that day was the result of a whole lot of other stuff. I'm not saying there was this direct cause or anything. But I think the whole thing wouldn't have went down the way it did if a lot of other stuff hadn't pushed Len to where he was. Is anybody looking into the other stuff?

FB: Well, we are trying to get a complete picture. We're trying. You said that it was Leonard's show, and that you and Cameron were only helping out?

CE: Right.

FB: Do you think that if you and Cameron had refused to help him, that Leonard would have gone to the school that day?

CE: What's that supposed to mean? I don't know what he would have done if things were different. He had something in his mind to do, right? He brought the guns and things to do something. So I guess he would have done it.

FB: When Leonard did anything, he did it with you or Cameron, it seems to me. He got angry with you, and with Cameron, but he apologized to you to get you to come to the school with him. Do you think he needed you for moral support? That's what I'm asking.

CE: Look, check this out, okay? I've been used before. My mother used me to help her run her life. My father borrowed money from me. My stepbrother ... well, people use people, and that's right up front. If Len was using me for moral support or to help him get his thing going, then that's what he was doing. What I'm trying to do is to get by—not even get over, just get by. Okay?

FB: I understand what you're saying. Let me ask you one last question. On balance, do you think you actually liked Leonard?

CE: With Len I was part of something—a little group—and maybe that's better than liking somebody.

FB: I don't see how it could be better if the "group," as you describe it, is not functioning very well.

CE: Yeah, well, that's the difference, man. Len understood it.

FB: I think we can end the interview here.

CE: Whatever.

Madison High School Incident Analysis
Report IV—Interview with Cameron Porter
Submitted by Sheriff William Beach Mosley,
Harrison County Criminal Bureau

William Beach Mosley: Cameron, I'm not that experienced as an interviewer on this kind of a team, and I know you've been through this a number of times, so I'm going to ask you to help me out as much as you can. I want you just to tell me what happened as best as you recollect. Then if I have any questions concerning what you say, I'll bust in and ask them. Is that fair enough?

Cameron Porter: I guess so.

WBM: Okay, I'm ready, you're ready, and the tape's rolling. Let's get to it.

CP: Starting from when?

WBM: I'm going to be concentrating on the incident, as they've been calling it, so why don't you just give me what you can leading up to it.

CP: The seven days before it happened?

WBM: If you think that works.

CP: Well, Len and I had been apart for a few days over Carla. Carla is this girl we had been friendly with, and Len found out that she had been molested by her stepbrother. Her real parents were split up. I think her mother was a waitress, something like that. Anyway, she was living in a trailer with her dad, who was a drunk, and she got molested. Len took her records from the clinic and scanned them into the Circuit, which is the school's newspaper on the Internet. I thought he was wrong big-time to do that and told him so. That's why we weren't speaking for a while. Then he called and told me that he thought I was right and that he was really sorry he had done it. He asked me if I wanted to go to his father's job with him to get some money.

I said okay, and he picked me up at my house. He said he wanted to go buy some fuses. So we started over to where his--

WBM: Just a minute, what kind of fuses was he going to buy?

CP: He had this idea of blowing up a Dumpster at school. The thing was to wait until one day when we wanted to leave early, then set off an explosion in the Dumpster.

WBM: With what? What kind of device did you have to do that with?

CP: He had mini cans of soda filled with some powder we got from firecrackers.

WBM: Cherry bombs? The little gray ones the Army uses?

CP: Yes. And then he downloaded some information from the Internet on how to fuse them up with a timer.

WBM: So you got the fuses and then what?

CP: No, we didn't get the fuses. We went down to where his father worked, and this guy said that we should come back later. Len didn't like that and said he wanted to see his father right away. We went to the garage area, behind the dispatch shed, and saw his father being chewed out by his boss. The guy was all over Len's father and Len's father was, like, squirming and making this little grunting sound. It was funny-- not funny, but weird. The sound was weird. We watched that for maybe a couple of minutes--I wanted to leave right away but Len was like frozen to the spot--then he took my arm and we left. He was really upset, not just mad but like out-of-his-mind mad. He was breathing hard and stuff. I knew he didn't like the way the boss was screaming at his father. But I didn't know why he was having trouble breathing. That's the way Len was sometimes. He would go off and you weren't sure exactly what it was about.

WBM: So you didn't get the money for the fuses and you never bought them?

CP: Right.

WBM: Where did you keep the canisters you had made up?

CP: In school. In the boiler room.

WBM: Are they there now?

CP: They might be--I don't know. I haven't thought about them.

WBM: Let's hold this interview a few seconds while I make a phone call.

. . .

WBM: So you were at his father's job. Then what happened?

CP: He dropped me off and went home. I guess he went home, I'm not sure. He didn't come to school the next day, Wednesday, but he called me in the evening and said he was in the Army, special forces. I didn't believe him at first, but then I did. He said he had been thinking about terrorists and how they had gotten away with attacking New York. He said he heard that what was really going down in Afghanistan and Pakistan was that the special forces were on the ground and going from door to door, killing anybody who even looked like they might be a terrorist. He said I should join too.

WBM: Were you thinking about it? About joining the Army?

CP: Not seriously. We had spoken about it before. Len was saying it was like starting all over again. But then he started slamming Carla. He called her a fool and a

	slut. Tulsa girl, that's what he called her.
WBM:	That's where she was from? Tulsa?
CP:	No, Tulsa is "a slut," only spelled backward.
WBM:	Yeah. Okay. I see that. Go on.
CP:	He said he was going to put her on his enemies list. So he was up and angry at the same time, which was unusual. Usually he was mad when he was down, but not when things were going right. So I couldn't read his mood. He said we should try to pull a chain on her. I just let him talk and he was talking about a mile a minute. He got back to what he was going to do in the special forces, maybe be a weapons specialist.
WBM:	What did he mean by pulling--did you say a chain--on the girl?
CP:	Both of us having sex with her.
WBM:	Were you both pretty active in that department?
CP:	I wasn't.
WBM:	Go on.
CP:	The next day he called me again.
WBM:	What day was that?
CP:	That was Thursday. He was really depressed.
WBM:	He was in what you've described as one of his "dark" moods?
CP:	Dark? No, he wasn't going dark, he was just depressed. He was way down. Way down. He's

not the kind of guy you feel--the only time
I ever felt sorry for Len is that time when
he was getting pushed around on the
football field--I felt sorry for him because
I knew how he felt. I had been there. But
when he called that Thursday and I heard
him talking, he was so down I felt sorry
for him. He said life wasn't working for
him anymore. I felt bad because I had
slammed him for slamming Carla. You know,
sometimes things happen and you blow them
up big-time and you should just let them
slide. That's what I was thinking when I
was talking to him, that maybe I should
just let things cool down for a while. I
don't mean to just totally chill with it,
but to back off a little.

Okay, that's Thursday. Friday he's back up
again. He told me that he had spoken to
Carla and they had made up. He said she
was going to help him do something big. He
wanted me in on it too. What he said he was
going to do was to get into school on Monday
and write "Stop the Violence" in his own
blood on the walls. It was on the walls. The
police even photographed it.

WBM: What did you think of him doing that?
CP: I was mixed on it. The idea was deep, right?

You write "Stop the Violence" in your own
blood, it's like using God's voice to say
something. But I knew that if we did that,
there was a chance we could be in big
trouble because of the thing with the court
before.

WBM: That would be the church-vandalizing
incident?

CP: Yeah.

WBM: I swear I don't know how people can do
things like that. You wrote on the wall
then, too?

CP: Yes. And part of the judge's decision was
about us keeping out of trouble. I wasn't
sure what would happen if we got into
another vandalizing thing. Especially with
it being in the school.

WBM: Why especially with the school?

CP: Church. School. A big organization. You get
into more trouble with that kind of deal
than you would with a small deal.

WBM: So you said no?

CP: I said no and he blew up. He said I was
like a traitor, something like that. I had
betrayed him. He called me Judas and then
started ranting some stuff that I didn't
understand. I felt screwed around. I mean,
I was sticking up for Carla and everything,

and now Len and Carla had made up and I
was the guy who was outside. But on one hand
it was all right because Len was getting mad
more and more and I was getting a little
nervous about him. So Saturday, that was the
next day, I decided just to lay low, and
maybe keep some air between Len and me.
What I wanted to do was just slide until
graduation. I wanted to graduate. I was just
going to keep my mouth shut and my eyes shut
and go about my business.

WBM: You were a senior. Had you been accepted
into any colleges?

CP: I was accepted at the University of Chicago
and Indiana, but my folks wanted me to go
to a local school to save money.

WBM: So you were just going to stay low until
graduation time?

CP: I didn't want to get into any confrontations
with Len, or Carla.

WBM: See no evil, hear no evil—

CP: Something like that. But thinking back on
it, I know it was still eating at me. I
went down to the basketball court to play
some ball and there were some guys I
knew, older guys, and I played with them.
I didn't do anything much in the game and
they started getting on my case, calling

me "white boy" and stuff.

WBM: These were Caucasians?

CP: No, they were black. Guys who worked around town and played ball on weekends. Some of them knew that I had played for Madison, so they had to show me up. That kind of thing.

WBM: When you play sports, you always want to knock off the big guns, don't you? If a guy plays for a big team and you don't, it's kind of natural for you to show what you got. Don't you think?

CP: Yeah, but I guess I wasn't in the mood or something. Then I went home and got into a big thing with my father.

WBM: What was that about?

CP: Same old stuff. I was reading a magazine, *Metal Hammer*, and he said I should be reading something useful. He reads the *Financial Times*, stuff like that. It's all about who you are and what you can prove about yourself and how come I wasn't more like him. That's what it's all about, really. I should be like him and be an advertisement. That's what he wanted. As far as he's concerned, I should even throw away my name and just say I'm Norman's son.

WBM: Did you speak to your mom that night?

CP: She was away at some sort of convention in Atlanta for people who sold office supplies. She got back Sunday. I didn't want to talk to her anyway. She didn't want to get involved. She said her place was to be--how did she put it?--supportive of me and my father. She was going to be involved around us and not between us, or maybe it was involved between us and not around us. I don't know. What it meant was don't come talking to her about anything if it didn't involve money or shopping.

  Sunday, he, my father, asked me if I wanted to go shoot some hoops. I knew it was supposed to be some big father-and-son thing and I was supposed to smile like some kid in a cereal ad, but I wasn't having it. I said I didn't want to shoot any hoops. Then he started running his mouth about how when he reached out to me I always turned him away . . .

WBM: Go on.

CP: Then he caught an attitude. I had an attitude too. So I went out to the library and hung there most of the day, just trying not to think. Sometimes I wish I could just not think. Then I went to the movies. When I got home, my parents were out. There was a message from Carla on my phone saying to call her.

WBM: You have a separate phone line from your folks?

CP: Yes. I called Carla and she and I just talked about things, and I asked her why she had got back with Len. She said that there was all kinds of violence going on in the world and what we were doing, getting mad at each other, was a kind of mental violence. And I said that being mad at Len for hurting her was not violence, and she said that it was. She said if you held it in, it became part of you and that it was always there ready to come to the surface.

We talked for way over an hour. Maybe over two hours. We talked about Len some, but mostly we talked about how our lives were going. Neither of us was whoop-de-doing it up. She even asked me if I thought we should make love, that you couldn't be violent if you were making love.

WBM: But wasn't there some violence done to her with somebody making love to her?

CP: Yes, but I think her head sort of vibrates in different directions about that. Once she even told me that it was probably her fault.

WBM: Did her case ever get into the court system?

CP: No, she never reported it.

WBM: Oh.

CP: So after Carla and I talked, I decided to call Len.

WBM: Did the young lady actually suggest that you and her make out?

CP: Not exactly. She just said it in a roundabout way--something to do to get away from the violence. I didn't think she meant she was going to do it or anything.

WBM: Did you think it might mean that?

CP: No. Maybe. I was going to keep it in mind.

WBM: Okay, so you called Leonard?

CP: I called Len and I said I was in. He told me to meet him at the school in the library and to bring some red paint. I told him I didn't have any red paint and he said black would do. I wasn't sure if I had any black paint either. Anyway, that's what I was supposed to do. But when he said to bring the red paint, I figured he had backed off doing the sign in blood. That sort of meant--I thought it meant that nothing would go down too serious.

    So then comes Monday. I got into school at about twenty minutes to eight.

WBM: How did you get in? Wasn't it locked at that time except for the teachers' entrance?

CP: You can always get in through the basement. They don't lock the basement, so if there's no one around, you can get in through the storm doors near the generator in back. I went in through there and went up the stairwell. I was pretty nervous. I had made up a story to tell if I got caught, about how I had to do some painting. I had found a small can of dark-blue paint in the garage and I was carrying that and a paintbrush.

WBM: In your family's garage?

CP: Yeah. When I got to the library, I looked in and saw Len looking out of the window. There was a duffel bag on the floor next to him. I went in and said hello. He told me he was going to paint on the walls of the library. He asked me if I wanted to cut him to start the bleeding. That's what he asked, if I wanted to "start the bleeding." I said no. Then he opened the duffel bag and pulled out the Kalashnikov. That's when I started panicking. I asked him what the rifle was for, and he said to hold off people until he had painted enough signs. I was still freaking out. I said that I didn't want any part of any rifles, and he pointed the gun at me and cocked it. I wanted to

run but I was too scared to move. I thought
he was going to shoot me. Then he laughed,
the way he does sometimes out of the side of
his mouth, and pointed the rifle down. He
said that Carla would get there any minute
and I should start painting signs in the
hallway. He told me to take one of the guns
from the duffel bag.

WBM: How many guns were in the duffel bag?

CP: I just saw one, the AR-18. There was
clothing in the bag too, and a lot of ammo.

WBM: Okay. What did you do when he told you to
take the gun?

CP: I said okay, because I just wanted to get
out of the library and think. I left the
library with the brush, the gun, and the
paint can. When I got outside, I painted
"Stop the Violence" on the wall across from
the library. I was shaking. Then I looked
back into the library and I saw Len's arm
was bleeding badly. He was painting on the
media board. He was painting "Stop the
Violence" and "Amos 8:3." I got even more
freaked.

WBM: Did you know what that meant at the time?
Amos 8:3?

CP: No idea, man. I tried spelling Amos
backward, but it still didn't make any

sense. I didn't know it was from the Bible.

WBM: Okay. Then what happened?

CP: Then I decided to get out of there. I just knew it was going to be bad news. I went down the hall to the exit across from the physics lab. I got there just as Carla came through the door. I told her we needed to split big-time. She saw the gun and asked me what I was doing with it. Then Len was yelling down the hall at us and I was trying to pull Carla into the stairwell and she didn't know what was happening so she pulled away. Then Len shot a blast at us and knocked out the glass from a display case. The glass shattered and blew all over the hallway and Carla screamed. I turned and saw Len headed toward us, and I jerked Carla's sleeve and we started running down the stairs. I was yelling that Len had guns and was bleeding and everything but I knew it wasn't coming out right. Len started shooting down the stairwell and bullets were flying every which way. I got off the stairs--they're open all the way down--and I was really into a panic thing. I saw the fire alarm and smashed it with the butt of the rifle. It went off and it was like the whole world was filled with noise. Carla was crying and breathing hard like she was having an asthma attack or something. There's a broom closet on the second floor, and I pushed her into it and told her to keep still. Then I went down the hall toward the front staircase. Len came onto the second floor and I shot at the wall next to him. He ducked back into the stairwell.

WBM: How far was he away from you at that time?

CP: All the way down the hall. It's a long hall. He was screaming at me and his arms and the front of his shirt were all bloody. I was afraid to go any farther down the hall because I didn't know if I would have the nerve to shoot Len if it came to that. I was still shaking and I ran into a classroom. When I was in the classroom, I thought I had made a big mistake. He could come into the room any minute. I got behind the last desk. They're not solid desks, so I knew he could see me if he came in. I was kneeling and aiming toward the door. The window was open and I heard all this noise outside. Screaming. I looked out the window and I saw kids running, dodging between the school buses. I saw two people on the ground; one was moving a little, the other

one was still. I heard shots coming from
somewhere, and I knew it had to be Len, but
I couldn't tell where the shots were coming
from, if he was on the second floor or if he
had gone back up to the third. All this
time the fire alarm was still ringing. I
didn't know what to do, or if Carla was all
right. I just crouched on the floor and
waited. Once in a while I would look out
the window, but I was really too scared to
move. Then I heard police sirens, and when
I looked out, I saw SWAT guys all over the
place, and they were heading toward school.
There were fire trucks outside too. I put
the gun down. I didn't want the gun in my
hands anymore. The SWAT guys came into the
building. One of them looked inside the
classroom I was in. I called out to him, and
he pointed his rifle at me and told me to
stand with my hands up. I did, and it was
over.

WBM: It wasn't over. A student was killed on the
spot; a number of other students were
wounded; and a lot of kids are going to
have this buried deep in their minds for a
long time.

CP: I know. I know.

WBM: According to the records, you didn't agree

139

to an interview with the investigators,
either from the SWAT team or the sheriff's
department, right after the incident. Why
was that?

CP: I was too upset even to think, let alone
talk.

WBM: Carla wasn't too upset to talk.

CP: That's what I heard.

WBM: When did you speak to your parents?

CP: About an hour later, when I calmed down
some.

WBM: They found Leonard upstairs under one of
his "Stop the Violence" signs. You know that,
right?

CP: Right.

WBM: Carla didn't see Leonard bring the rifle
into school, did she?

CP: No, sir.

WBM: And she didn't see who was shooting out of
the windows. So that part of it is left up
to you to report, isn't it?

CP: It's the truth, sir.

WBM: Well, Cameron, I believe it is the truth,
but it's a hard truth and a tragic truth,
and one we're all going to have to live with
for a long, long time. I appreciate your
help.

CP: Thank you.

WBM: One last thing. After that morning, did you
     ever speak to the parents of the boy who was
     killed in the parking lot?

CP: No, sir, I couldn't bring myself to face
     them.

WBM: I can understand that.

Madison High School Incident Analysis
Final Report and Dissent
Submitted by Dr. Jonathan Margolies,
Superintendent,
Harrison County Board of Education

Dissent: Special Agent Victoria Lash

As we review the tragic events of last April 22, it is the opinion of the Board of Education of Harrison County, based upon the Board's independent investigation, the various reports of the School Safety Committee, police reports, grand jury findings, and interviews with the principals involved, that the circumstances and nature of the incident did not constitute a clearly avoidable episode. Indeed, it is the majority opinion that, using the highest level of security acceptable in a school context, the events of April 22 were neither predictable nor preventable. The salient facts of this matter involve the entry into the school building and access to that property in the vicinity of the school, including the parking lot, athletic fields, etc., and the peculiar mind-set of the shooter. Inasmuch as all school property is public and cannot be denied to students who legitimately attend Madison High School, it is deemed unreasonable to expect that the weapons should or could have been detected while merely in the vicinity of the building. The students on school property were protected under the Fourth Amendment against unreasonable searches.

The actual entry into the school was a deliberate breach of security, but it is to be pointed out that students are often allowed into the building prior to the opening bell under present policy, and also that the events relied not upon easy access to the building but on the intent of those making entry. In fact, the entry into the building did allow one of the students to sound the fire alarm, which probably saved lives and prevented injury.

In previous police inquiries the Harrison County Criminal Bureau has determined that the intent of the shooter was his alone and that the other students found in the building had not intended to do bodily harm to any other student. It is therefore reasonable to conclude that the unfortunate death of one student and the several injuries were the work of one individual and that the responsibility for that death and those injuries were his and his alone and were not aided in any way by negligence, errant school policies, deficient procedures, or lack of adequate safety conditions.

Signed: Dr. Jonathan Margolies

Signed: Dr. Franklyn Bonner

Signed: Dr. Richard Ewings

Signed: Sheriff W. B. Mosley

Dissent:

Although the legal obligations of Harrison County might have been technically fulfilled, it is clear that not enough was done in the way of ongoing threat assessment prior to this incident. The points to be considered are:

- Previous errant activities by Mr. Gray
- Known threats made to a teacher by Mr. Gray
- Known abuse of drugs by Mr. Gray
- Known incidents of bullying directed toward Mr. Gray
- The availability of weapons to the students.

Mr. Gray was the proverbial "ticking bomb" waiting to go off. His needs were conveniently dismissed at every stage. His reaching out for help was also ignored, and there was no co-ordinated concept of threat assessment. A conclusion that threat assessment is not the responsibility of the local governing body is an invitation to re-create these events. Mr. Gray, by most accounts, seemed to be a young man who did not attract a great deal of sympathy for his many troubled causes, but it is the situation, and not the personality, that needed to be monitored and controlled. The "tragedy" is not only the death of two students and the multiple injuries of other students, but that any chances of prevention were lost in the morass of shifting responsibilities and legal considerations. Although it is admittedly difficult to monitor individual reactions to what are increasingly common circumstances, the protection of other students and the general population demands more than was done here.

Victoria Lash

Signed: Victoria Lash

Madison High School Incident Analysis

Appendices

Appendix 1. Newspaper Reports

Madison High Shooting Spree

Harrison *Courier*, April 22

A tragic shooting interrupted classes at Madison High School today as two students were killed by gunfire and six were wounded in what police officials are calling a murder and suicide.

One suspect, a seventeen-year-old senior at the school, was captured with an automatic weapon. Police said that he had not been charged in the killing.

The names of the dead and injured have been withheld pending further investigation.

"How could this happen here?" asked Sylvia Whitan, a distressed parent. "This isn't some depressed area."

The Harrison County School Board declined comment.

Madison Star Slain in Weird Cult Shooting

Daily Press, April 26

Brad Williams, 17, has been identified as the young man killed in what appears to have been a cult killing in Madison last Monday. The coroner's office reported that the teenager had been shot multiple times and had, perhaps, been sought out in what initially appeared to be a random act of aggression.

"It was the most terrible thing I've ever seen," said fifteen-year-old Grace Majewski. "Everybody was screaming and we heard Brad calling out for help, but there was nothing we could do."

Police found bloody writings on the school walls, and there was talk throughout the school of "dark happenings."

Leonard Gray and Cameron Porter
Named as Shooters in Madison Case

Westword , April 25

Two teenagers, one a cult member, were named today in the shootings at Madison High over the objections of their parents and the attorney for Porter, Frank Maffei.

"We have to remember that no formal charges have been made," said Mr. Maffei. "And there is a presumption of innocence until a jury, not the press, reaches a conclusion of guilt."

Both students were found in the building after the incident, which left two dead and nine wounded. Mr. Porter could be charged as an adult, but the sheriff's office refused to tip its hand at this time.

Brad Williams, who was killed during the incident, had received scholarship offers to four colleges, according to the school's guidance counselor, James Aumack.

Several students who did not want their names revealed said that the cult to which Gray belonged was influenced by a number of underground rock groups.

Rites Held Same Day

Harrison *Courier*, April 28

Two young men who never could get together socially were buried on the same day in starkly contrasting ceremonies.

Brad Williams was interred at Holy Name cemetery yesterday. Most of the Madison High School student body turned out for the funeral of this bright all-state athlete. Mr. Williams was described in a eulogy by the Reverend Arthur Bright as "an example of what America should be about."

Leonard Gray was interred at Green Meadows cemetery. His parents and close friends of the family attended the rites of the accused assailant and suicide. Father Lucien D'Amato of St. Bridget's asked the attendees for love, sympathy, and understanding for the Gray family.

onorary

Grand Jury Says No to Porter Charges

Companion, July 7

A Harrison County grand jury failed to issue an indictment against 17-year-old Cameron Porter, accused of being an accomplice in the April 22 shootings at Madison High School. Porter, Carla Evans, and Leonard Gray were in the building when the shooting occurred.

"We'll probably never know what really happened," said 15-year-old Erica Rigby. "And that's just wrong."

Michael Williams, father of slain scholar Brad Williams, said that he would not rest until he had found a full measure of justice. "You don't send your kid to school, teach him the right things to do, to have it end like this," he said.

Appendix 2. Police Report

Harrison County District Attorney
Verified Investigator's Report

Report made by:	Date:	Charge:	File No.:
Mike Lardner, Det.	April 24	Homicide	44-F-0923
Suspect:	Suspect:	Victim:	Victim:
Leonard Gray	Cameron Porter	Brad Williams	

SYNOPSIS OF FACTS: 17-year-old Brad Williams killed by shots fired from 3rd-floor window of Madison High School in Harrison County.

DETAILS:

Brad Williams was 17 years of age and attended Madison High School in Harrison County.

On April 22, shots were fired from a third-floor window or windows of Madison High School. The results of the shots fired were minor gunshot injuries to several students and the death of Brad Williams.

The fire alarm was set off at approximately 7:57, eight minutes before the start of school. The fire alarm signal is loud enough to be heard from a distance of one quarter of a mile outside the school on a clear day. The alarm was answered by the Harrison County Fire Department's Engine Company 16, Emergency Squad B, and Ladder Company 9.

At approximately 8:03 the Harrison County Police Department received a 911 call of shots fired at the school. Responding were officers Pete Vega, William Davis, and Elizabeth Kelly, in three different squad cars.

When the above-mentioned officers reached the school, they came upon a scene of panic. Students were running, some were hiding under vehicles in the nearby parking lot, and others were lying on the ground, apparently injured. Automatic fire was detected coming from a third-floor window. This firing was sporadic, and it is not clear if all of the shots fired came from the same window.

159

It has been ascertained by the county Criminal Bureau that all of the slugs recovered in the parking lot were fired from two weapons found on the third floor.

A SWAT team was assembled and transported to the scene, arriving at the same time as emergency medical vehicles. Wounded victims were removed when possible. One victim, Brad Williams, was shot multiple times as he lay on the ground, apparently even after he was deceased.

The SWAT team entered the building at 8:33. Three students were found in the building. Cameron Porter, 17, was on the second floor. There was a weapon in the room with him, a loaded AR-18. Porter was searched, handcuffed, and taken into custody and the weapon taken as evidence. Carla Evans, 17, was on the second floor in a closet. She was searched by officer Elizabeth Kelly, handcuffed, and put in the custody of EMT personnel, who transported her to Mercy Hospital for treatment of shock and emotional trauma. On the third floor the body of Leonard Gray, 17, was found. There was a Ruger pistol by his side as well as a Kalashnikov. From the positioning of the wounds it appeared that Gray had placed the muzzle of the rifle in his mouth and self-inflicted a fatal wound. The Ruger was taken as evidence, as was the Kalashnikov. In the library a Galil and numerous ammunition clips were found. The weapon and the clips were taken as evidence.

The SWAT team cleared the building by 11:00 A.M. School was declared closed for the day, and trauma counselor Spring Myers set up headquarters at Mercy Hospital.

Cameron Porter was too upset to be interviewed immediately by investigators and was placed in a secure holding pen at the Harrison County 2nd Precinct while his parents were on their way to the scene. When his parents arrived, he agreed to be interviewed and gave a detailed statement to the police. He was held as a material witness for 24 hours before being released on bond by application of his family's attorney.

Miss Evans was also held for 24 hours after she arrived at the precinct from Mercy Hospital, also as a material witness, and was then released on bond by application of her family attorney.

160

While no charges involving the actual homicide were filed against Cameron Porter, the investigation is deemed to be open in respect to his participation. It is to be noted that Mr. Porter was allowed to watch the television news report of the incident in the precinct and knew of Mr. Gray's death before consenting to the interview.

Submitted by Detective Mike Lardner

Appendix 3. Miranda

Statement of Waiver of Privilege and Miranda Warning

I understand that any statements I make in the ensuing interviews are not privileged by doctor-patient relationship. These statements are made voluntarily and with full knowledge that they may be used against me in either a criminal or civil prosecution.

I further understand that I have the right to remain silent and the right to an attorney. I understand that I may exercise these rights at any time during the interviews.

I further understand that I have the right to an attorney. If I cannot, on my own, avail myself of legal help, I will be furnished an attorney by the State.

My signature affixed below is an acknowledgment of my understanding these rights as stated, and I have no questions about my rights.

Signed

Cameron Porter

Date

10/24/03

Witness *Sam Yeh*

Statement of Waiver of Privilege and Miranda Warning

I understand that any statements I make in the ensuing interviews are not privileged by doctor-patient relationship. These statements are made voluntarily and with full knowledge that they may be used against me in either a criminal or civil prosecution.

I further understand that I have the right to remain silent and the right to an attorney. I understand that I may exercise these rights at any time during the interviews.

I further understand that I have the right to an attorney. If I cannot, on my own, avail myself of legal help, I will be furnished an attorney by the State.

My signature affixed below is an acknowledgment of my understanding these rights as stated, and I have no questions about my rights.

Signed

Carla Evans

Date

10/27/03

Witness *Whitney Menger*

Appendix 4. Diary or Journal Found in the Home of Leonard Gray

Dec. 25

Halle-Yulemas! Halle-Yulemas!

I got a check from HIM and this lousy book from her. Mom says I should keep a diary and that it would help me to keep my thoughts together. I told her I didn't have any trouble keeping my thoughts together. I just let them run through my head, scurrying like little rats wherever they want and me listening to their squealing their little rat songs, or are they wheeling and dealing right along with everybody else??? What I did not say was that I was having trouble keeping my LIFE together in this EFIL, stupid house. Oh, yes, she also told me I should try to smile more. It's all the useless garbage of her life. Smiles and Miles of limes and rhymes that she calls good times as she

smiles from across her tiny Cosmos.
Wonderful. I can imagine her sitting at the
kitchen table looking at some stupid
women's magazine that says you should
encourage your teenager to keep a diary.
And to smile more. Maybe I will write my
thoughts in this book, only it will be my
die-ary. And as for the smiling bit I have
an alternate idea. I'll use this book (red for
Yule-mas!) for my non-smiling list. List +
Enemy = Smile? Nyet! Number 1 on the list
is Brad Williams, a royal jerk. Or maybe a
pickle-headed gherkin? I wonder if his
whole family are gherkins and him just the
dilly of the lot—or does he represent an
advancement?????

Cameron called and he sounded like a
lump in the dump and not at all miserly
with his miserableness. His cousins came by

From Chicago on their way to somewhere. Why are people always pretending to go somewhere when there is no place to go?

January 1

HE started the year off at the top of his game, telling me how I couldn't do anything right and how great he had been when he was my age. According to him he was at least perfect, numero uno. Numero Uno— A = 1, the first letter, K=11, the 11th letter, 4+7=11. Numero Uno is 11111 = AK-47.

HE made a New Year's re—solution to cut down on his cigars. What was the old solution? He should cut down on his breathing. Mom is such a sheep, so she made a re—solution to lose 7 pounds. Why would she want to lose weight? For HIM?

He wouldn't see the loss. What can he see? You can't see if all you have is 1-1-1-1-1's.

They played a Spiritual Beggars jam over the loudspeakers at the Mall. Right in the middle of all the Xmas drivel. Not bad and there must be a metal freak on the mall staff. There were so many humanoids running around buying symbols and toasters and symbols and ornaments and symbols and anything else that wasn't nailed down.

Jan. 5

Saw Carla at the clinic today! She didn't see me but I saw her coming out of a group session. She left in a Big Hurry and got the 23 bus downtown. One of the guys she was talking to was Frank Gazzara. He sucks big-time but I think I can talk to him.

Mom says that I should lighten up! What should I cut off to make myself lighter? Maybe a leg or an arm? When she sees the bloody stump and asks me why I cut it off I can finally tell her that I'm just obeying my parents. Har-Har.

Blow-off at the old Madison ranch. The whole nine yards. Fine shards of sarcasm. Letter home, lecture, pointing digits by mental midgets. Bad boy, Mr. Gray! The school is an unsafe environment, giving me mucho headaches. Making my rat thoughts scurry faster and stay longer, and their squealing scrapes the plaster along the hospital-green walls.

Problem: HE says that I am holding myself away from the world. What a dense! Here I am living in this house and I can't do anything in it without HIS permission. I can't do anything outside of it without the permission of the whole world. They have given me a role. I am acting in this farce and I still can't be the leading man, even in my own life. The crowd looks up at me, the Ubermensch, teetering on a wire above them, pushing my cage before me. Jump! Jump! They are yelling at me like the crowd of fools they are. Should I jump down to be with the masses, or stay isolated? I told Cameron that I felt isolated and he said that we are all isolated, prisoners in our own skins. Is Pyramus really this wize? Or does he just guess, dreaming up his own world?

There are always too many pills and not enough pills. Did God invent pills on the 7th Day?

Dr. Franken at the clinic is so gullible.

Yesterday was my final day in the program and he asked me if I had ever dreamt about S-E-X. He tried to make it sound soooo casual. I should have told him that I dreamed about making it with penguins, or something like that. I bet he loves to hear what people dream about. I saw his wedding band. He probably goes home and tells his wife everything he hears in his office. I told him that sometimes I dream about making out with girls at Madison. Then he asked me if I ever dreamed about any of the teachers. The camphor on my head is making me drowsy. But the scratching of his pen keeps me alert. Leonardus Grisleum. He had me categorized. I have him categorized. Perfidious Profundum!

I dream about body parts, I vesper

whisper to my rats. Parts without faces is truth without traces. Is dreams without schemes. Is fable without labels.

He said he was going to summarize my case. He asked me if I wanted to hear his summary, and my rats said that if he wanted me to cool out he should winterize my case, but I said yes and nodded so he would be prodded to do what he was going to do no matter what I said. He announced that I wrote on the walls of the church as an act of rebellion and that I needed to channel my energy into positive activities. THE MOVING FINGER WRITES ALONG THE WALL AND THEN THE REBEL LION EATS IT!

Toosday
Spoke to Frank Gazzara at the Inconvenience store. He's supposed to be

really smart but with a loose screw or two, which is why he can't use his college degree. I don't think he's that smart. I told him I was having trouble and asked his opinion about joining a group. He said sometimes a T group helped. I asked him what kinds of things I would talk about in a T group and he said anything that bothered me. Then I tried to caress his cerebellum for information about his group and he slunk into his turtle shell and waved his fat little hands around the edges. I asked him what good was a group if he could only talk inside the group and he shrugged and looked more off than moron. I told him I knew a girl in a group and that her name was Carla. He moved his head up and down and said he knew her, that she was in a group at the clinic. Righteous.

In history today they asked us to imagine ourselves as a historical figure. Right away hands shot up, volunteering to be Georgie Porgie Washington and Abie Baby Lincoln and Mr. Napoleon Bony-part. Then essay assignments were handed out according to who you wanted to be.

I am Quasimodo. Quasimodo turned inside out with my lips too red and my legs too short and my hump slung across my back as I turn into the brisk wind that lifts the dirt from the street and drives it into my face. Through the wind and the flying debris I hear the bells ringing. Who rings the bells? THAT IS MY JOB!

Thursday
Suspended for one week! Just trying to go from amateur Zacs to the Pros. They

want me to cool it and don't see when I'm going there. Will atone by 40 hours of Mortal Kombat and 40 Hail Marys!

Got into it with Drab Brad, the beastie buoy in the sea of strife. He is a living testament to the NEED for abortion. He got into my face and all I could think of was how he needed to have his chromosomes rearranged. He is numero uno on my <u>Smile? Nyet!</u> list.

Cameron said I should have hit him back. What CAN a Cameron possibly know about violence? Nothing! But can I teach him?

I wouldn't give the Brad Moroff the satisfaction of stooping to his demented level.

The freakin' car sounds more like the washing machine. HE says that a vacuum hose is probably loose and causing the vibrations and says that I should be enough of a man to fix a simple hose. So—that's what makes a man, changing hoses. If I change my hose will I be a man? Was that how man began? Did a monkey look down at his hose, see it needed to be changed, and suddenly became a man? Was the monkey surprised? Disappointed?

Ran out of magic pills and called Dr. F's office. Three months ago he said he was going to switch me to Sumpin' Nu and Wonnerful but, like the fool he is, he didn't give me a prescription for anything. I told his nurse to have him call me and she called back and said that he had called in the prescription to the drugstore. He's too busy to call me. I'm hoping it's something good for an O pious brother or at least an O pium brother or maybe he's

figured out another METHod to ease my
tired brain.

Another Day, Another Holler
Cameron and I in the parking lot. Face to
face with the escapees from the Planet of
the Apes. They grunted and scratched and
beat their chests and laid hands upon our
Holy persons. I took names, writing them down
furiously in my mental book of Reckoning.
Cameron said he was going to the Principal's
office. I tagged along to hear our fuzzy-
faced Princienemy tell C that we should
ignore the creatures from the Planet of the
Apes. They are EXPRESSING themselves.

February
Does February feel bad because it is
short? Because it is so cold?

Looked up uses of traz on the Net. Takes three weeks to kick in but superior side effects will have me rising to any occasion.

After a lousy supper of murdered bovines HE was complaining that they were laying off people down at his job. He said they would probably have to keep on the kneegroes because that's what they usually did. He went on about how the kneegroes were getting everything. "The ones who ain't in jail or on welfare, which is most of them." His cigollisms abuse me.

February 9

My thinking to write something every day lasted ONE day. Took the Ruger to school today. It felt good banging against my leg.

Stopped at the Army Recruiting Office

after school. Just for a laugh. I took a test and knocked the socks off the recruiting sergeant. He said I was the smartest person to come into his office. He had me fill out a questionnaire and asked me what I wanted to do in the Army.

I should have told him I wanted to kill people, but I didn't. Instead I pussied out and said whatever the country needed me to do. It sounded kind of noble but my rats still tittered.

What I could do is be a Seal, except I don't swim that well. I could be a sniper. SNIPER = Penis R us!

He asked me what I thought of the D.C. sniper movie. I didn't see it but I know what they did was stupid. A Bushmaster is not an AK-47, even with a tripod to steady the barrel.

If I went into the Army I'd probably never come home again. Maybe I would live on post for a while and even marry a foreign girl. No Asians, though.

Spoke to the Guidance Counselor without Cam today about getting harassed by the Mongrel Hordes. He said the Viking way of life meant that I should pick up my shield of maturity and Deal With It. Don't be a whiner, he said.

If the punch flies, "Deal With It!"
If the crunch cries, "Reel With It!"
If the french fries, "Feel With It!"

Some people are good at making piles, words or turds, it doesn't make a difference. Just open an orifice and let them out. What is the matter with you, Mr. Gray? If you had more spine, you wouldn't whine. Are you a gayGray?

On the way home and listening to my rats scratching around my head, I cut off a truck and the guy started laying crap on me and giving me the bird from the window of his Big Mack. I added a whole generic breed to The List.

Valentine's Day
At Cameron's pad and me and him goofing on this Saint Valentine Dude. The Saint of sending out cards? The Saint of buying candy? What??? His mom telling me how much their new swimming pool will cost.

I am feeling very good and think that

going into the Army will be a good thing. Mom will do her boo-hoo bit about me not going to college but I don't give a crap. If HE opens his mouth I will give him a shot HE won't forget.

They went out to dinner. This is a new thing because She was saying that HE never took her anywhere. When they were gone I took out HIS Kalashnikov and tried out the sniper sling position. Not too easy. But I could feel my pulse and tried timing my trigger pull to go between the pulses. I am going to buy my own piece. Maybe I will go to a gun show and wander through the camouflage forest, trying to guess the name of my fair and deadly maiden. Will it be Kalashnikov? Could be.

Called Cameron just to talk, to hear the

sound of my voice echo through my room. To hear how rational I sound when I am speaking to Other. Cameron is okay, but he still has faith in the SYSTEM. He is yakking about what to major in when he gets to college and not hearing me tell him that is all about the future and doesn't he know that the future is already past and the only thing to know is that tosorrow, and tosorrow, and tosorrow creeps like the pretty rats that race from gray to gray. Cam thinks he has bought into the future with his grades and shades, but the market is all a charade and the buying only a sale sold by an idiot, a bull that's round and hairy, pignistying nada. I will have to DRUM the truth into him, and if he is too backward to get it I will have to RE-DRUM the truth into him so he will understand it.

My rats are getting busier. If they run backward will they be stars?

Monday, depressing

Came downstairs and hear her crying and sniffling and HIM screaming at the top of his stupid lungs about her not backing him up when he got into some stupid argument last night at Lacy's. HE thinks Lacy's is a big deal because all the rich white guys go there and that's what he wants to be. HE had got into a discussion about immigration and She had the nerve to correct him. She said he had changed his mind, that just a week ago he was all for immigrants. That was true when he wanted to justify hiring Mexicanos to load and unload his trucks down at the depot, but it wasn't true when he needed to suck up at Lacy's. I put a star next to his name on the list. I hope HE sees it. I'll tell him that it means I admire HIM so. Next week he will change again.

Why do I hate the weak? I don't hate the month or the year? But the weak creeps up and grabs me by the throat like slack the nipper, unclear through the foggy groggy streets of Whitechapel. Weak is always there, being obscene and not heard.

ANOTHER DAY!

How many days will there be!!!
Confusion = Cun Fu Zion = pain is the only real emotion. Everything else can be taken away. Love, happiness, joy can always be

taken away. Even old sadness can be dissipated if you pee enough ha-ha into it. But pain is pure. And the more pain the purer. And the Kon-phew-shun moment, that time-space continuum where pain almost reaches death, and you don't know whether you should reach for more pain and risk dying or turn back and deny yourself the high, is the new territory, the creative moment.

Spoke to Brad today. He said I was a worm. A worm? A squirm? A germ of a worm, squirming in the parking lot next to Brad's BMW? Cameron came by and one of the Frenchies grabbed him. Oh, how those Jacques are so quick to know who they can grab and who they cannot. Cameron stood up, looked into their faces, his courage transparent as he accepted the clear pane of their intimidation.

What to do? What to do? Took prescription for magic pills to pharmacy in Oakdale. In the car, waiting, I ask myself what I will do. And suddenly I am Sebastian, accepting the arrows of my fate, accepting the mean stares of Christians who are pissed because I am not the Savior.

Spoke to HIM about taking karate lessons. HE says it is what the Orientals do. They hop around in bedclothes and scream at each other, says faux papa. Not like his stranger ranger daze when men were MEN. At the next nexus with Rabbid RabBrad maybe I will bring kryptonite and mime the Book of Revelation and show him that I am gameo and let him unscramble the message.

I have bought a gaw-juss weapon. It lies beneath my bed like a secret lover, quiet, powerful, waiting to work its magic. I lie above it, quiet, powerful, waiting to work my magic. The rats are quiet.

March the Whatever

It is so cold outside. I saw a homeless woman begging downtown. I would have given her a lift if she were going somewhere, but she wasn't. They never go anywhere. Cameron and me in the lunchroom. Margaret Keller opening her fat mouth and talking as if she had more than the half a chicken brain that runs her CPU. She is a moron and too dumb to menstruate straight.

Another day, they are piling up!

Took Ordo Saggitae out to shoot. So far the members are Cameron, Carla, maybe Paul, and maybe Walter Klubenspies, who is the most suspect. Matthew 19:14.

There comes a time. Times come. Times roll down the avenues like dust devils, like tornadoes disguised as dust devils, like summer thunderstorms disguised as dust devils. Time comes. The noise from the shooting is unreal. It doesn't feel like dying flying out of the hole but the K piece gets super busy muzzle muscling retri and bution all over de place and the noise of it and the feeling of life jerking in your hands separates you from anything anybody can say except howdy retri and howdy bution.

I think Cameron is afraid of guns. I think

he is afraid of me, but he admires me. I
don't blame him. He'll be the only person I
will write to when I am in the Army
killing the enemies of the United States of
America. What annoys me is that I know HE
will want me to write to HIM and will
brag about me being in the Army. HE
fought in the jungles of Colombia against
guerilla drug lords in the '80s with the
Rangers and in Yemen against Iraqi Special
Forces. But if I go into combat it won't be
any clandestine operation. It will be
straight up and against the enemies of the
U.S. of A. I will be a killing machine. A
death machine. Full metal jacket. Full met
hell jacket. Full met hade jacket. met
hade=death + me. Mine will be the shot
heard round the world. I imagine a shot
going round the world. I will shoot, then I

will let mine enemy stand in front of me and point his weapon at me. I will dodge his bullet. Then, As The World Turns a full 360 degrees, it will kill him. I could sigh with delight as the gray matter roils and boils. Or is it die with the light? Or is it dis little light of mine?

March 12th

Always on a Tooesday. Shooting with the Patriots. One man, one vote. One gun. One shot. Cameron was upset to see a black target. Martin Luther King. When Cameron is not around they say Martin Luther Coon. I don't mind. I told Cameron not to mind. As long as you know the enemy you can deal with him. He wouldn't shoot at it even though everyone said it was just a joke. Cam got quiet, fell into himself, his eyes wide, like he had lost his balance and was helplessly spinning into the bottomless pit of his own darkness. Ooooh, I know that place. I know that place.

We left together, but not together. We are all isolated, alone. Trapped between 12 and whatever THEY call legal. Cam was being sad about Martin Luther and I was feeling mad because he was feeling sad and I don't think I can feel sad anymore. On the way home I thought about that, that I don't ever feel sad anymore. Maybe it's the laughing of the rats that keeps my spirits up.

Dr. F asked me if I have ever been in love. Where is love? Is there a door? Do you have to buy a ticket to get in?

At the Ranch. Brad called me a faggot.
He pushes and pushes into me. What does he
want to know? I'll just tell him and then
we can play another game. Who am I? I'm
the white nigger with the right trigger,
the dog barking at the edge of the
universe, the last moonbeam before
daybreak. Hey, Brad. Hey.

Ides

Was Caesar tired? I am tired. I dreamed
about shooting. Me with the most powerful
gun in the world. I shot and the bullet
traveled past a dozen countries and three
oceans and killed me. I told Cameron my
dream. Some kid over in Wausau decided his
part of the fight was over and got on
Suzy's side. Me and Cam talked about it,

what kind of nerve it would take. Right away the camera man got deep. He asked me what I thought about it, if I thought I would miss the future, the holy Nextus. No, I don't think so. The desert doesn't mourn the rain.

An article on the Net says the 30-round clip has changed warfare. They are wrong. A 30-round clip only represents 9 seconds of mayhem.

April

I remember when I was 6 and marched to the beat of a child. Over the last decade of my life I have lost the cadence and de-generated into de-cadence. That is what the decades are about, the slow march to de-cadence.

Fried Day

I woke up feeling close to everyone, but to no one. Shooting again. Me, Pyramus, and Carla. The Trinity. We shot at targets in shells. I was only touching in the dark. Sometimes everybody touches in the dark. You touch to see what you can stand to touch, what you can stand to feel with your fingers probing parts you never thought you could probably probe.

What are they? Prehistoric things with prehistoric shells covering their thingy bodies, it was not the hare-racing happening that Carla was screaming about. Carla boiled the hate up in me. She twisted her deep Goth lips. Deep Goth black lips on her white face and looked ugly at me. She scraped my bones with her evil eyes. I looked at Pyramus and he was looking shell-shocked. It was her fault. He follows whatever pulls at his ginger heart and I know that if she is going to be so offal then he will wollof and won't be kcab until she comes kcab. There was so much going on that I couldn't get up an explanation. It felt like Brad standing in front of me asking me why I was so lame. But if Carla and Cameron turn against me, what will I do? It's her fault. How could I not recognize her as the Universal Slut? The US that makes me the outsider? How could I not see that? Am I blind? What to do? What to do?

Saturday

What to do! Yea, and verily, too. I have copped the evil hag's record from the clinic. I have copped and slopped it over to the Circuit and she is reviled and revealed as we are all reviled and revealed! Now I know all and all will know all. The Tulsa girl is the wize child who knew her own brother. She is a victim! A vice-tim! An MCVII to a T! I am boiling over. I do not like myself but I can't stop. The rats are hissing in my ears. I don't know the tune.

Afternoon

HE slaps Mom again. She cries in a corner and has no rage to turn against him. He walks the house, imagining himself to be the captain of some ship, woofing at his crew. Her eye is bleeding. The eye is the entry to the soul, and her soul drips blood. She cries, still waiting to appease him, waiting to slip back into his good humor.

He talks to me about fishing, and even

as he talks about renting a boat I know that I am the chum that he hopes will drive the sharks to frenzy. I am Isaac under an eager knife. Later, they go off to their darkness and grunt. My part in the play is small. I come onstage, smile, and fall on my face. I run off to the canned laughter of an audience who wait for Better Things.

Still April the Desperate

The Jacques are on Carla today, and I bleed with her. She hates me but I am rolling around the floor in the track of her pain. I am hating myself and think of nothing but Suzy, alone against her attackers. But, still, the weaker Carla looks, the more I hate her. She is a whore

and Cameron is a he-row, but she knows it
and he doesn't. He asked me if I had heard
about Carla's case being on the Circuit. I
said no. But then I talked with one of the
Jacques and he asked me and I said I had
put it on and he laughed and I laughed and
he laughed and I laughed and . . .

They killed turtles! How can life work if
you can't kill turtles? If turtles are what's
important? Turtles are a path. They are a
path that leads you to forever outside.
They are a path that leads to the road not
taken, the goad not taken, the load not
shaken from your skinny white shoulders.

Again, and Again
Today I peeped through my eyeballs
into my brain and saw the whirlwind

spinning through my mind.

The Office called me down today and said I had doubled my prescription of a DANGEROUS drug. They wanted an X-planation! I told them I was just trying to raise my depression to a cee-pression or even a bee-pression, so I could raise my GPA and become Collage material. Then they could cut me up and I would FIT IN.

APRIL, the Cruelest Month
IF CRUEL=LUCIFER
Carla's pain is my pain. I am the cause and I can't take it back. It weighs on me. It has its way with me and my tears drip both curds and whey, but it is Cameron's anger that is crushing. I wish to God that I were not in this place, this framed breath, this life.

April the ∞

I'm sitting here on the edge of hope
Looking through my cosmic telescope
At a world looking back at me
From the wrong side of eternity
And the only clue that my poor brain finds
Is a world I've already left behind
I've already left behind
I've already left behind

She was right, this die-ary is yoosful.
I'm sitting here MIR high and mighty and
writing down the words to Downthesun's
new jam and everything is peaced to
perfection. Only none of it works and all
of it works and there's no freakin'
difference between the two.

Two p.m. A call from the world. Dude

wants to part with a righteous Galil for a mere four bucks fifty. Got my number from the Pay-trots club. Mom is breadless. Can the Galilean turn out enough loaves and fishes for the Galil? Called HIM to skim scam the necessities and he says to come on down. Made an excited call and begged to get on the good side of Pyramus. Told him about the Galil and he demanded his pound of flesh but he threw me a crumb of friendship upon which I feasted and fawned. I will pick him up to go and watch me fawn before HIM for the money. The Galil will be wurf it!

It Draws Near

Now everything is clear. Now everything is clear and the world is clear and it doesn't work. It's falling apart. I am dumb numb. Visions of HIM standing there looking like a pink jellyfish and listening to his Brad Boss chewing on HIS brain while HE got smaller and smaller and sinking through the cracks of the he-meant cement floor and sniveling with HIS whole body, his hole body sucking up the crap of the moment and being the me that nobody noes and everybody knows with their grinning and winning. There was me standing with my head down, wearing my pink father's skin like a body bag while the rats recited passages from The Waste Land. Then I was out of there and running with Cameron behind me asking me what was wrong and me telling him that I just needed to outrun myself before I caught up with me in some dark alley and I was sure he could understand that. He didn't but he came up with the 4 bucks fifty for the Galil.

And what happened when HE came home? What did the moving finger write upon the wall? HE storming around the house like supermouse and screaming his violence and Her running around catching it as it bounced off the walls. Then his hands slapping and crapping all over her and me running downstairs angry at the top and 13 stairs down shaking like the fool I am. And HIM transferring the hole of nothingness from HIM to Mom and onto me for the perfect double play.

Nothing is working. I am on the wrong end of eternity and I've got to leave this tired world behind. Cameron is still together. My main ginger man. I told him I was sorry about dissing Mary Magdalene and he ran down his Amens about how it was WRONG because she had been THROUGH enough and all the time I am thinking about what has been THROUGH her because she is just a slut and a crap and a sorry grass skirt that falls beneath the Dominations and Powers of any THINKING man and even though I am cool with what I am saying I know that I am on the cresty edge of hope and the hope is crumbling, man. It is crumbling. I look at Cameron and hear his voice and he sounds like the roar of the mighty ocean busting out my eardrums but I can't understand the words for all the noise that's going on.

And what I need to do if I am to survive is to go Under Cover. More and more people are peeping my hole cards. I think they might be reading my thoughts. I have got to cover them. Maybe I need to act fast before they know my route and cut me off. Or maybe I need to leave this world behind, sail across the world to Afghanistan or Pakistan and discover a new world.

April, Still April, How Tired Can I Get

Went back to the spit-shined folks at the U.S. Army Recruiting Office. Sergeant Razor Sharp said I looked like a Fine Young Man and I said he looked like a Fine Young Man and I took his Fine Young Man test and he said "You are a smart Fine Young Man" and we sat down and went over my Military Options. I told Cameron and he asked me why I wanted to go into the Army and I told him that I needed to kill all the Evil in the world to get the balance back again and he looked at me and gave me a constipated smile and when I read his face I did not see wisdom. What I saw was a smile that he wore like a minstrel mask.

What I will do is clearer now. When one life does not work then you pack your bags and go to another life, jump over to the road not taken and dance down that road until you get somewhere you recognize. Down the road not taken and all the time burning the bridges behind you so the hounds can't follow.

Cameron says that he has not seen me so up as I am now. I am really set at what needs to be done so maybe I am up and set or set up or upset. All I know is that I am singing in my mind. Over and over the same words.

I'm sitting here on the edge of hope
Looking through my cosmic telescope
At a world looking back at me
From the wrong side of eternity
And the only clue that my poor brain finds
Is a world I've already left behind

The words and the tune run interference
and nobody, but nobody can read my
thoughts, not even Cameron.

Still April, the Cruelest Month
HE is apologizing. HE has lifted HIS huge
head from licking HIS Brad Boss's feet and
the blood is back in HIS bowels so HE thinks
HE can put on HIS robes of graciousness and
all will be well. Mom scurries about smiling
and grateful. There is WEAKNESS and

IMPURITY in this house, it flows through the blood.

Still April

The Army has beamed into my mind with their microwave radar and read my thoughts. They called and spoke to Mom first and then to me, grinning over the phone as they spoke, saying that I lied about taking prescription drugs. They think they are clever but they are wrong. What did I say? What could I say? I put the rats on the phone and went to bed.

"Did I say something wrong?" Mom asked me.

She peered at me from the corner of her timid mind and asked me if she had done something wrong. She told them I used

drugs because IT WAS THE TRUTH, she said.
Was that wrong? TO TELL THE TRUTH? What
does she know about the truth? The truth
is that I am a brown paper bag filled with
maggots and foul wind and the stench of it
is floating in the air. And the only thing
that is left for me to do is to go even
deeper undercover until I can find a vynal
solution. I told her not to worry about it.
Not to worry at all.

April 19th
The months have days in them. I call
Carla and she says she is shocked to hear
from me. I am so deeply undercover that I
do not recognize myself. Deep. I have a
plan. No, not a plan, a statement. What I
see, what I should have seen all along, is
that I have to create the real me. They

have been creating me. HIS Brad Boss created HIM. It is the Brads of the world that create us, that beat us into existence, that make us their "things." Without the Brads of the world we would be Dick and Jane and whoever showed up in the textbooks. We would live by the word and the word would be the freaking Constitution or whatever has us all created equal and with Unalienable Rights while we run around pursuing happiness. But we don't live by the book or the word or the rules but by the lures of power and <u>intimidation</u> when we can't even see Tim and nobody knows where he lives. Now I have to create a real me, a me that is laid-back and that is Beyond beat-down alley. A me that is strong, and brave. A me that is not afraid to have a voice.

Carla understands. Blessed is she among women. We talk and she talks and she fills in the gaps where there are gaps. We are both victims wandering through familiar territory.

April 20

Can't get hold of Cameron and I am desperate to talk to someone. Don't want to risk losing Carla, who is going to deal with me. I am half sick with excitement and half sick with despair. But I know, finally, that there will be a solution. A solution: a liquid, either volatile or not, in which a foreign substance is dissolved. What foreign substance can I dissolve in blood? Carla says that I should try poster paint. That way we can write our epistles with a flourish. We can tag the world with a demand to Stop the Violence.

Stop the Violence!

Smile? Nyet! Don't smile, Cameron. Go on with your Judas Ginger self.

April 20, Again!

I have held Mr. Ruger's invention close to the Temple of Doom but it doesn't work. The hands have betrayed me, the transition is too great. There is no Squeeze and SQUISH. There is only Freeze and WISH. I have to burn the bridges to Eternity. I'm too weak to leave the walk into the darkness, to go Gentle Into That Good Night. I need a guide across the River Styx. Maybe Brad will consent to guide me. It's about time for him to do something good for me. I am tired. I listen for the rats,

and hear the high pitch of their squeals.
They sense SOMETHING IS GOING TO HAPPEN.

April 21

Pyramus is In the House! His stupid
father pushed him once too many times
and at the right time and at the time to
emit and admit the fact that he is
defeated. We can rock Gethsemane if only
they can stay awake. Can I trust them to
go all the way? Can I take them? It's
going to be hard, but Pyramus is in the
house, and I know I can go on. I CAN GO
ON!

April 22

Everything is ready. My room is clean.
The Mom person will be pleased. I have

sent in my English assignment. It is a quarter past six, and I am having tea and toast for breakfast. The rats titter and squeak.

Appendix 5. Medical Examiner's Report

HARRISON COUNTY MEDICAL EXAMINERS OFFICE

Examining Physician Esther Balducci	Date: April 24	Requested By: Sheriff's Office	LG-1303
Gray, Leonard	Age/Race 16/Cauc	Cause of Death: Gunshot wound	Time of Death: April 22 9:03

STATEMENT OF FACT:

17-year-old white male found dead in the aftermath of a shooting incident at Madison High School in Harrison County.

FINDING:

The deceased, a 17-year-old white male, was found on the third floor in the above-mentioned school. Cause of death was a gunshot wound with the point of entry being the hard palate. An exit wound was found in the left rear quadrant of the upper skull, the bullet having traveled through the brain. The wound is consistent with the subject's having placed the muzzle of the gun in the mouth and fired the weapon. Powder traces found on both hands indicate that the deceased had recently fired a weapon. Body position is consistent with the impact of the bullet.

Multiple superficial cuts were found on both the right and left wrists and forearms. There was blood on the fingertips of the left hand. Body was found beneath a sign, written in blood, that read "Stop the Violence."

CONCLUSION: Death by self-inflicted gunshot wound.

Walter Dean Myers is the acclaimed author of *Monster*, the first winner of the Michael L. Printz Award, a National Book Award Finalist, a Coretta Scott King Honor Book, and a *Boston Globe–Horn Book* Author Honor Book; *The Dream Bearer*; *Handbook for Boys: A Novel*; *Bad Boy: A Memoir*; and the Newbery Honor Books *Scorpions* and *Somewhere in the Darkness*. His picture books include Jane Addams Children's Book Award winner *Patrol: An American Soldier in Vietnam*, illustrated by Ann Grifalconi; *I've Seen the Promised Land: The Life of Dr. Martin Luther King, Jr.* and *Malcolm X: A Fire Burning Brightly*, illustrated by Leonard Jenkins; and the Caldecott Honor Book *Harlem: A Poem*, illustrated by Christopher Myers.

He is the recipient of the 1994 Margaret A. Edwards Award for lifetime achievement in writing for young adults and the 1994 ALAN Award for outstanding contribution to the field of young adult literature. Mr. Myers helped establish the Walter Dean Myers Publishing Institute, part of the Langston Hughes Children's Literature Festival, and makes frequent appearances with the National Basketball Association's "Read to Achieve" program.

Mr. Myers lives with his family in Jersey City, New Jersey. Learn more about the author and his books at www.walterdeanmyersbooks.com.

Praise for THE DREAM BEARER

"This quiet, subtle story works on a number of layers with several themes—dreams, visions, home, community, and manhood. Moses's dreams offer no easy solution to David's problems, but they become part of him, add to his knowledge, strength, and understanding, and nudge him toward a renewed relationship with his father and an appreciation of the danger and the magic of Harlem."   —*Kirkus Reviews* (starred review)

"Throughout his nuanced examination of this unhappy family, Myers retains his usual gentle, plainspoken accessibility, making this a thoughtful book that will reach many young readers."
                           —*The Bulletin of the Center for Children's Books* (starred review)

"This is a haunting, sad, and yet hopeful tale of one boy's struggle to cope with his father's mental illness, and Myers makes David and his world come alive for the reader in deceptively simple yet poignant prose."   —*Kliatt*

Praise for HANDBOOK FOR BOYS: A NOVEL

"This is a book about community, about African American men recognizing the problems our youth face and beginning the healing process through mentoring. I've been waiting for somebody to write this book. It doesn't surprise me that Walter, who's dedicated to these young people, has written it."
                           —Nate "Tiny" Archibald, Former NBA Player and NBA Hall of Famer

"Once inside, readers will be hooked."   —*Publishers Weekly*

"This book is an important one for parents and teachers to share with their kids."
                                                       —*Black Issues Book Review*

Praise for BAD BOY: A MEMOIR
An ABA Kids' Pick of the List

"Myers is arguably one of the most important writers of children's books of our age. This glimpse into his own childhood is wonderfully valuable, fascinating, inspiring."   —*Kirkus Reviews*

"A powerful read that will reaffirm one's belief in the power of reading and writing. It will make the reader laugh out loud and sigh with satisfaction."
—*Voice of Youth Advocates*

"An ultimately hopeful, realistic, and inspiring story, especially of interest to aspiring young writers." —*Bookselling This Week*

Praise for MONSTER
2000 Michael L. Printz Award
1999 Coretta Scott King Author Honor Book
1999 National Book Award Finalist

"Chilling and engrossing." —*The New York Times*

"Tailor-made for readers' theater, this book is a natural to get teens reading—and talking." —*The Horn Book* (starred review)

"This riveting courtroom drama . . . will leave a powerful, haunting impression. An insightful look at a teenage suspect's loss of innocence."
—*Publishers Weekly* (starred review)

Praise for PATROL: AN AMERICAN SOLDIER IN VIETNAM
2003 Jane Addams Children's Book Award

"An unusual and gripping picture book set in Vietnam and geared to older readers." —*Publishers Weekly* (starred review)

"Highly effective and very important." —*Kirkus Reviews*

"Hard to forget." —*School Library Journal*